JEANMARIE,
with Love

JEANMARIE,
with Love

APPLE VALLEY
MYSTERIES

Lucille Travis

Baker Books
A Division of Baker Book House Co
Grand Rapids, Michigan 49516

Published by Baker Books
a division of Baker Book House Company
P.O. Box 6287, Grand Rapids, MI 49516-6287

Printed in the United States of America

Library of Congress Cataloging-in-Publication Data

Travis, Lucille, 1931–
    Jeanmarie, with love / Lucille Travis.
       p.   cm. — (Apple Valley mysteries)
    Summary: During World War II, Jeanmarie, Pearl, and Wilfred from Apple Valley Orphanage are hospitalized after a circus fire and, while exploring the nineteenth-century basement tunnels in New York City's Bellevue Hospital, they encounter a thief.
    ISBN 0-8010-4479-0 (paper)
      [1. Orphans—Fiction. 2. Circus performers—Fiction. 3. Bellevue Hospital—Fiction. 4. Blind—Fiction. 5. Christian life—Fiction. 6. New York (N. Y.)—Fiction. 7. Mystery and detective stories.] I. Title. II. Series.

PZ7.T68915 Jg 2001
[Fic]—dc21   2001025519

For current information about all releases from Baker Book House, visit our web site:
                http://www.bakerbooks.com

To Anna,
whose smile and loving ways
bring so much joy

Contents

Warnings

*I*n his office at the Apple Valley Orphanage, Dr. Werner put down his pen and glanced at the small clock on his desk. It was nearly midnight, and he'd have to be up early in the morning to see Miss Bigler safely off with her charges. With Miss Bigler in command he need not worry, since little escaped her sharp notice. A smile touched his mouth as he thought of the circuses of his own boyhood. He picked up his pen once more and added a last postscript. "Uncle Thorn, I meant everything I said above; you truly are the most generous man I know." Who else would have paid for an entire orphanage to attend the grand Ringling Brothers and Barnum and Bailey Circus and insist on remaining an anonymous donor? Dr. Werner stood and, satisfied that all was well, turned out the light.

In another part of the orphanage grounds, Jeanmarie lay in her bed in the girls' dorm; she felt a sharp stab of pain run down her side. Several times it had awakened her, and now she couldn't get back to sleep. Across the room Winnie snored lightly. Nearby the twins, Maria and Tess, huddled under their sheets in spite of the warm July night. What if she'd been a twin? Jeanmarie smiled and pictured another girl, like her, with brown hair in braids reaching past her shoulders. They'd be twelve together, mostly "skin and bones" Winnie would say, and this year all their old clothes would be too short. She wondered if her twin would have a straight small nose like hers. In her bed by the window, Pearl murmured something in her sleep. She might as well have said, "Hey, don't forget me." Jeanmarie sighed. They might not be twins, but they were as close as any real sisters. She listened to Pearl's even breathing, wondering if she was dreaming and wishing she was awake. In winter they'd pushed their cots together and shared their blankets. More than that they'd shared their dreams and secrets. Tonight Jeanmarie felt lonely.

Jeanmarie thought about her own mother who never came to visit. She remembered the day she'd come to the orphanage, scared and yet sure she wouldn't be staying long. Only she had. It all seemed so long ago, like a bad dream. In the dark Winnie mumbled in her sleep, and Jeanmarie smiled, then felt a sadness steal over her for Winnie, who'd never known a single relative. They were family now, all of them, and thanks to some donor, tomorrow they'd be off to the circus. None of them had ever been to one, and she was determined no little pain would hold her back. Her eyes felt heavy, but the burning in her side kept her awake. The sky was beginning to grow light when sleep finally came.

Miles away the circus workers were already up, preparing the great tent for the day. In the field behind it, near the performers' tents, angry voices rang out on the morning air. "Stay away from the princess; I'm warning you." The voice came from a tall clown in the doorway of a tent. A few feet from him one of the workers known as roustabouts raised a defiant fist in answer as he limped away. "Ought to be fired," the clown said, stamping inside with the morning bucket of water.

A small knot of workers had stopped to listen, waiting for signs of a fight. "This circus has enough trouble," one of them stated. "I don't like the feel of this weather," he said, turning away. "That tent roof ain't gonna take it much longer."

Beside him an older fellow signaled him to hush. "Can't tell when one of the bosses will come sneaking around. Talk like that'll only get you fired." His voice was low. "All on account of money, they done put that cheap stuff on the tent top. Wouldn't give you a nickel for it myself. Should've listened to old Mike's warning. One good match and the whole thing'd go up in smoke." Behind them the roustabout with the limp paused and looked at the huge circus tent with its high peaked roof. Moments later he headed to the mess hall with the others, anger still smoldering in his eyes as he thought of the clown.

ONE

Screams in the Air

*B*y afternoon a blazing July sun had turned the giant circus tent into an airless hotbox. In the center ring of the arena a large black leopard, his powerful muscles rippling as he circled the cage, refused to obey. Nearby other leopards moved restlessly on their perches. The young golden-haired woman trainer repeated her command. Swift as lightning the great cat in front of her swiped with his paw at the stick in her hand. Seated in the front row, Jeanmarie saw blood running down the trainer's arm. The woman stepped aside quickly and in a sharp voice demanded obedience. When the leopard snarled again it startled Jeanmarie, sending a stinging pain like sharp needles through her right side. She held her breath until the pain left. With the war still on, this might be the only circus she'd ever see.

Next to her Pearl whispered, "How can the trainer stay in there with that leopard? It's so dangerous. But it says here that the princess is the best woman wild animal trainer in the world." Pearl pointed to the circus brochure in her lap.

Jeanmarie nodded and felt a fresh stab of pain. The heat in the tent made her feel slightly nauseous. She glanced behind her at the rows and rows of people between her and the exit. Somewhere back there Miss Bigler, second in command at the orphanage, was sitting with the others in a reserved section where she and Pearl should be. But the only empty seats left had been these two in the front row. Beside her, Pearl nudged her arm. "Look up," she said. Jeanmarie leaned back and stared up at the high wires forty feet above.

Moving with the grace of dancers while the circus band played a soft waltz, the Great Wallenda family had climbed to the high wires to begin their performance. Suddenly the waltz music of the band switched to the booming sounds of "Stars and Stripes Forever," and as Jeanmarie watched, the performers came sliding down the ropes to the ground. But they were not climbing back up; they were leaving the arena by the back door of the tent. The master of ceremonies began blowing his whistle shrilly.

"What's going on?" Pearl said. In all three rings of the arena the animal trainers were driving the big cats toward the exits, prodding with chairs and cracking their whips. Assistants shouted at the animals to hurry them through the steel-barred runways that led from the collapsible cages in the rings to the cages outside the big tent. In the center ring, four of the leopards resisted every effort and refused to enter the steel runways with the others. Jeanmarie sat on the edge of her seat as the princess inched closer and closer to the lead leopard. Never looking away or losing the firmness in her voice, she commanded it to leave. The big cat did not budge and again swiped at her, while the others snarled defiantly.

The princess shouted, "Someone turn the water hose on these cats! Hurry; we've got to save them!" An assistant ran for the hose and turned it on the cats, forcing them to move. Jeanmarie stared, puzzled. This couldn't be a part of the act. She wiped the sweat from her forehead. It must be the awful heat. The animals didn't like it either. Something else bothered her, stung her eyes, like smoke. Someone outside must have a bonfire going. People were beginning to move restlessly in their seats.

In the general noise, the ringmaster called for attention. As the crowd quieted he said, "Ladies and gentlemen, please leave quietly; the show is canceled." Stunned, Jeanmarie turned to Pearl, whose face had gone white.

"Look," Pearl cried, pointing to the top of the side tent wall on the left near the front exit. "Fire!" Like an arrow a line of fire flew from the side wall across the tent top. The sudden sound of moving chairs, cries of "fire!" and screams filled the air. Jeanmarie felt as if she was watching a bad dream. From the bleachers some people threw down chairs to clear the way below and then jumped to the ground, only to stumble over the chairs. Horrified she watched women toss their children down and jump after them. The crowds pushing toward the main front exit found themselves cut off by the fire and a mad rush of bodies from every direction. Jeanmarie strained to see Miss Bigler but saw no one she knew in the mass of people pushing and climbing over chairs to escape. The next moment she thought she saw Wilfred, but he quickly disappeared into the crowd. Miss Bigler was nowhere in sight.

Pearl clutched Jeanmarie's arm. "We've got to get out of here!" she cried.

But how? Jeanmarie could barely hear her in the din. Everywhere around them, from the bleachers to the ground floor rows, hundreds of people were trying to get to the exit. She coughed as the spreading fire sent down smoke and cinders. There was no way she and Pearl could ever reach the main exit in time.

People had started to pour onto the arena in front of them, looking for another way out. Jeanmarie felt herself pushed forward as a wave of bodies pressed against her. Pearl had hold of her arm, and the two of them were swept into the arena toward the animal runways.

Ahead of them, connected to the cages in the rings, the three-foot-high, steel-barred runways blocked the way to the back door of the tent. Jeanmarie stumbled, but Pearl, to whom running came as easily as breathing, was still holding on to her and pulling her along. Jeanmarie managed to get her balance and keep running. Men, women, and children all seemed to be heading straight toward the steel barricades. Pearl kept propelling the two of them parallel to the runways, heading away from the crush of the crowd and toward the side wall of the tent.

Jeanmarie could hardly breathe, and the pain in her side was forcing her to slow down. "Help us, God," she prayed. Her voice seemed lost in the terrible noise and panic around them. They had to get over the barrier and out before the whole tent collapsed. The solid steel runway had no openings. They would have to climb it and then push their way through to the back exit.

Overhead the roar of the fire flamed, and to Jeanmarie's horror, great patches of flaming canvas fell like burning blankets, some of them on the crowd. She could feel the blistering heat on her face. Her feet and legs seemed to belong to someone else, but somehow she was running. There were fewer people now as Pearl continued to pull her toward the side of the tent. They were nearly there when the sound of a giant tent pole falling sent fear racing through her. Cinders and debris were everywhere. She stopped to slap at a spark on her skirt as Pearl also slowed to a halt to brush away ash from her hair and face. On the other side of the animal runways the circus band, which had played on and on, stopped. The bandmaster, face blackened and uniform singed, fled with his men as another of the great poles crashed to the ground with a sickening sound.

"No time!" Pearl shouted. Clutching Jeanmarie's sleeve she pulled them toward the tent wall. Jeanmarie had no strength left. Her eyes stung and her throat burned with the taste of hot smoke. The terrible sound of cries and screams, the smoke, the fearful noise of crashing poles tore through her, and suddenly she knew what Pearl meant— there was no time to climb the barrier; the whole tent was collapsing.

Jeanmarie barely saw the heavy chunk of wood that fell and struck the edge of Pearl's head, knocking her down. In a second she had fallen on top of Pearl, who lay unmoving. Jeanmarie shook her. "Pearl, wake up. We have to get out of here. Wake up; I can't do this alone!" she cried. Any minute the tent would come down. She couldn't leave Pearl, and she could never make it over the barrier with her. There was no one here to help them. "Please, God, help me!" she cried. Why had they come so far to the side of the tent running alongside the steel runway instead of climbing over it with the rest of the crowd? A voice inside her said, *The runway goes out the side of the tent.* Could she crawl under the side of the tent? They were close to the tent wall. Pulling Pearl by the feet, she crawled backward, staying near the hot steel cage. Where the runway went outside the tent the canvas was loose enough at the bottom for her to get under. Using all her strength she pulled Pearl until they were both out of the tent. She didn't let go of Pearl or stop crawling backward even when she could feel grass underneath her legs. She kept going until they were no longer near the fire, kept going until she couldn't crawl anymore.

The sounds of trumpeting elephants, screaming cats, and jabbering monkeys filled the air. Animal cages were all around them. Almost near enough for Jeanmarie to touch, a cage full of monkeys gripped the bars and reached out small paws to her. Pearl lay pale and still on the ground in front of her.

"What's this?" The voice above her made her look up. A tall clown in baggy pants and a torn coat knelt down by her. "Let's have a look here at your friend, shall we?" he said gently.

Jeanmarie nodded. She licked her dry lips and coughed. Tears ran down her face. "I don't know why she isn't waking up. She has to. Please, can you help us?"

"Now, don't you worry, Miss." Pearl's eyes fluttered. "See there, your friend here is coming 'round or my name's not Willie. That's a nasty gash on her head. Must have hit her head enough to knock her out." As Pearl's eyes opened then closed again, the clown patted her arm. "Here you go, Missy. Weary Willie never makes a bad bet, and I'm betting you'll be right as rain soon. Speaking of rain, I have just the thing we need right now. You lie still while I fetch water and a cloth." He stood up and in spite of his great flapping shoes ran quickly toward one of the animal cages. In a moment he returned with a pail of water and a cotton cloth.

Wringing the cloth out after dipping it in the water, he laid it across the top of Pearl's head. "There's a lot of folks needing help just now. Do you think you can stay here with your friend?" he asked, looking at Jeanmarie. "Someone will be along for you soon. I'll come back here to see how you're doing as soon as I can. But I just bet someone's looking for you two beautiful young ladies right now." He patted Jeanmarie's head. "The cold cloth should help."

"Thank you, sir," Jeanmarie said. The clown smiled and left. Jeanmarie bent low over Pearl. "Does it hurt much?" she asked.

Pearl opened her eyes. "Not too bad, but why is it so dark here? Where are we?"

Jeanmarie stared at Pearl. "You have a cut on your head from a piece of falling wood, and we're safe outside in the field where they keep all the animal cages. We're both pretty black with soot. Don't worry, my eyes stung for a while too. Do you want me to wet the rag again?"

Pearl pushed herself into a sitting position, and the rag fell to the ground. "What's over my head?" she cried. Waving her arms and hands frantically she felt her head and the air around her. "Where are we? Why is it so dark? I can't see you." Panic filled her voice. "Jeanmarie, where are you?"

Jeanmarie grabbed Pearl's hands. "I don't understand!" Jeanmarie cried. "I'm right here." A stab of fear cut through her. Pearl couldn't see! Trembling, she placed Pearl's hands on her own face and then on her shoulders. "It's me, Jeanmarie, and we're sitting outside on the grass. It isn't dark; it's light."

"But I don't see anything!" Pearl cried.

Jeanmarie stared at Pearl's face. "Your eyes are all swollen the way they get every time you have a bad case of poison ivy. It has to be from all that smoke and soot in the fire. A cold, wet cloth over them should help." Jeanmarie wet the cloth and placed it against Pearl's eyes.

For a few moments Pearl held the cloth against her eyes. When she removed it she sat very still, her eyes swollen but open. Her cracked lips moved silently, and then, in a whisper so low Jeanmarie had to bend close to hear, she said, "It's never been like this before. Something's happened. I can't see anything!"

TWO

The Sound of Sirens

"Jeanmarie? Please, don't leave me!" Pearl's voice rose in panic.

"I'm right here," Jeanmarie said quickly. A chill ran down her spine. She raised her hand in front of Pearl's face and moved it back and forth. "Can you see anything?"

"Nothing. It's all shadows," Pearl said, rubbing her eyes.

"Don't," Jeanmarie said, grabbing Pearl's hands. "Rubbing them could make the swelling worse. There's got to be soot or smoke or something in your eyes. Miss Bigler will know what to do when she comes. They must be looking for us." She pressed Pearl's hands tight. "And until they find us we'll hold on to each other." She could feel tears on her face. It didn't matter. Pearl couldn't see them.

The noise of fire engine sirens, ambulances, and police cars filled the air. "There's so much going on,"

Jeanmarie said. "It won't be easy to find anyone in the crowds. There's probably a place set up to help. We should ask the man who stopped to help us where we're supposed to go."

"Was he a policeman, the man who was here?" Pearl asked.

"No," Jeanmarie said, realizing suddenly that Pearl hadn't even seen him. "He's one of the clowns, the one called Weary Willie, with the black face and big white mouth that always looks sad. We saw him in the grand parade, the tall one with the big white handkerchief."

"I think I remember," Pearl said. She turned her head restlessly. "I can still feel heat. Tell me again, where are we?" Her voice rose anxiously.

Jeanmarie loosed a hand and patted Pearl's arm. "The air is hot and humid, but we're away from the fire in a field where the animal cages are parked," she said. "You can hear the racket they're making. I guess they're scared too. It doesn't look like there's anyone around the cages but us. I think everyone's gone to help." The image of crowds running under the burning tent top flashed before her. "Oh, Pearl, there must have been thousands of people inside the big top," she cried. "I don't know how many were hurt. Everything happened so fast, it didn't seem real to me at first. If you hadn't run to the tent side, I don't know how we'd have gotten out." She didn't want to think about it.

Pearl clutched her hand and whispered, "You're the one who dragged me out."

Jeanmarie sniffed. "I didn't know what to do. God helped us both."

Pearl squeezed her hand. "When we were running in there, I," she hesitated, "I didn't know if we'd make it." She sniffed and said in a lighter tone, "I never knew you could run so fast."

"All it took was a fire," Jeanmarie added. "Let's try the wet cloth on your eyes again. I'm sure it will help." She wasn't sure. At least the gash on Pearl's head had stopped bleeding, though there was a definite lump.

"Thanks," Pearl said. "Do you think I could sip a little of that water? My throat is parched."

"I'll hold it close, and you can scoop some in your hand." She guided Pearl's hand to the pail. On the third attempt Pearl managed enough to satisfy her. Jeanmarie gulped some of the murky water herself. Her mouth tasted like ashes.

No one had come looking for them, and the clown had been gone far too long already. Farther down the long line of animal cages she could see some of the circus crew running to help with the crowds that were overflowing the field where the tent had been. The circus brochure called it the biggest circus tent in the world, six hundred feet long, two hundred feet wide. It no longer existed.

An uneasy thought pulled at Jeanmarie. What if the clown had forgotten them? In all the chaos how would anybody find them? "Maybe I ought to look for a policeman to help us," she said to Pearl.

"No, please don't leave me," Pearl begged.

"Can you walk holding on to me?" Jeanmarie asked as she placed Pearl's arm on her shoulder and put her own arm around Pearl's waist. Pearl's swollen eyes were mere slits in her face, and Jeanmarie knew she couldn't see.

"Yes, if you tell me where to go," Pearl said. "Let's find the others, please."

Poor Pearl; Jeanmarie knew she had no clue of the milling crowds of people covering the fields. To go that way meant being lost in the crowds. Out of the reach of the fire and beyond the animal cages stood a row of small tents, and she headed toward them. Someone there could surely help them.

But tent after tent was empty, flaps hastily flung aside and left open. As Jeanmarie peered inside the next to the last one she saw a man bending over an open trunk. She was about to call out when he slammed the lid and stood up holding a long necklace of sparkling red stones in his hand.

"Worthy of a princess," he said, shoving the necklace into the pocket of his shirt.

"Please, sir," Jeanmarie said from the entryway.

He turned with a startled look on his face. Before she could say more, he rushed rudely by them, pushing them aside, and ran off, limping as he went. In seconds he had disappeared behind another tent.

"Oh," Pearl gasped, stumbling.

Jeanmarie steadied her. "Sorry," she said. "I don't know who that was who just rushed by us." She looked up as Weary Willie the clown and the young woman trainer, the princess, came toward them from the opposite direction. Willie waved at them. The princess was leaning on his arm, and as they came closer Jeanmarie saw long ugly scratches on her legs and the dark, red-stained cloth wrapped around her right arm. "So there you are!" the clown said loudly. "I told Princess we'd find you, and here you are looking for us."

"Sorry," Jeanmarie said. "I thought you might be too busy, and it would be better if we looked for help since nobody would know where to come for us."

"Such a bruise," the beautiful young woman said. Her voice was soft and full of sympathy as she gently touched Pearl's head wound with her good arm.

Pearl flinched. "What's happening?" she cried. "Jeanmarie?"

Jeanmarie caught Pearl's hand tightly in her own. "I'm here," she said. "It's Willie the clown, and the princess is with him." She looked up at the clown. "Please, can you help us? Pearl can't see, and I don't know what to do."

The princess's eyes were wide as she looked first at Jeanmarie and then at the clown. "Poor child," she said softly. "Your eyes are swollen nearly shut." Gently patting Pearl's arm she soothed her. "And that nasty wound on your head needs attention. I myself have some scratches from my poor cats today. They must have smelled the fire before we knew of it. Nana, the big cat, misbehaved badly, but our good doctor friend will know what to do. He is my very favorite doctor, the one all of us circus folk go to when we are close to New York City's Bellevue Hospital." She put her arm around Pearl's shoulder. "You are a brave girl to bear your pain so well. We have a car waiting for us, and we can take you both." She turned to Jeanmarie. "I'm sure your parents would want medical help for you quickly. We will get word to them through the police as soon as we have you safely in Dr. Hamilton's hands."

"We're from the Apple Valley Orphanage group," Jeanmarie said. "I think Miss Bigler will be looking for us, or Dr. Werner, the superintendent." The clown gave a sad look, which was exaggerated by his thick makeup, and patted Jeanmarie's shoulder. This wasn't the time for Jeanmarie to explain that she wasn't really an orphan, though she lived in the orphanage just the same as if she were one.

"Well then," the princess said, "we will leave word for them both."

Jeanmarie saw a shadow of pain cross the princess's face. "I saw how brave you were in the leopard's cage when they wouldn't mind you. I hope they're all safe," she said.

"Yes, thankfully. I'm afraid this has been a terrible day for all of us, my cats included. Now I will just get my bag, and we will go." She went to the trunk, opened it with her good arm, and pulled out a brown cloth bag with long strings attached to it. "I should have kept this with me. Most days I do," she said as she searched the inside of the bag. Suddenly her eyes grew wide. "My mother's gift is not here!" she cried.

"Must have left it in the trunk," Willie said. He helped her look. "Sorry," he said, the frown on his painted face deepening. "No luck."

A sudden sharp pain made Jeanmarie gasp, and Pearl cried out. "It's nothing," Jeanmarie whispered.

"Leave this to me, Princess," Willie said. "I'll come back later. The girl needs a doctor to look at her eyes, and you need help for that arm and those scratches before infection sets in."

The princess hurried to Pearl and Jeanmarie. "Forgive me," she begged. "How thoughtless of me to keep you both standing here waiting. Of course we will go right away. Come now. Can you walk, child?" She gently touched Pearl's hand.

"Yes, I'm fine as long as Jeanmarie leads me," Pearl said. With the clown helping Princess and Jeanmarie holding Pearl's hand, they left the tent and headed for the street. Ambulances and police cars seemed to be parked every which way, sun glinting on their metal hoods. The noise and heat made Jeanmarie's head spin. Her side throbbed with pain. Ahead of them a sleek, black Ford waited near the end of the field, and its driver waved as they approached.

The driver, an older man with thick, gray hair, shook his head. "We've got one passenger already. I found him holding Joe's little dog, the one he uses for the hotdog bun trick. Guess the boy saved the dog from burning up, but I think he's got a broken arm out of it. Spunky kid, alright. Hated to see him wait around for the ambulances. They're full up with burn victims. It's the worst disaster I've ever seen." The driver shook his head as he held open the car door. Inside, his face sooty, his hair singed, glasses sliding down his nose, and his left arm tight against his chest, Wilfred sat holding a small brown and white dog on his lap. The dog yipped then licked Wilfred's face.

"Wilfred!" Jeanmarie exclaimed. "How did you get here? Where are the others?"

"I don't know where anyone else is, and how I got here is a long story," Wilfred said. "And right now I don't feel up to it." Jeanmarie climbed in next to him, trying not to sit too close to his injured arm.

When they were all in, Willie slid into the front seat. "Belle-vue, Lou," he said. "Better make it fast; we've got a mighty sick lot here." At that moment Jeanmarie's stomach lurched, sending pain shooting through her. She heard Wilfred say, "Hey, watch it," just before a dizzy blur turned the world black and she heard no more.

THREE

Beds, Basins, and Bandages

*R*eady," said a voice somewhere above Jeanmarie. A bright light was glaring down into her eyes, and she was lying on a hard surface. Her head felt woozy. She'd been poked and questioned in the hospital emergency room and wheeled onto an elevator; all she wanted to do was close her eyes and go to sleep. "Just breathe deeply," said the voice, "and you will be fine." Jeanmarie struggled to avoid the thing that suddenly covered her face; then she did as the voice said and breathed deeply.

She felt light as a feather and looking down saw that she was standing on one slippered foot on the back of a white stallion. From far away someone called her name, and she tried to open her eyes. She felt so sleepy that it took her a while. When she could finally keep her eyes open, she saw the face of a Chinese woman above her. "How are y'all feeling?" the nurse asked. Jeanmarie closed her eyes again. Where was she? How could a Chinese nurse have a Southern drawl?

The soft Southern accent cheerily continued. "Y'all had your appendix out, and that old anesthesia makes a body feel thirsty. This cracked ice will help. It's best not to drink anything just yet." Jeanmarie stared at the nurse. She'd had an operation! Bits and pieces about the fire and the trip to the hospital came back to her. But even while she tried to remember, she drifted off to sleep again.

The rattle of tin basins and the announcement "Time to wake up" roused her. "Morning." A young nurse who introduced herself as a student stood next to Jeanmarie with a basin in her hands. "You feeling better?" she asked.

"I think so," Jeanmarie said. "Feels like I lost a day somewhere."

The student nurse laughed as she arranged the pillows behind Jeanmarie. "You slept most of yesterday," she said. With her help Jeanmarie managed a mouth wash. Exhausted, she let the nurse wash her face and comb her hair. Sitting propped up against two pillows, she tried a few spoonfuls of Jell-O and looked around in awe at the huge hospital ward.

The ward was ten times larger than the orphanage dormitory. Rows of beds filled the room from end to end. Nurses in starched white uniforms hurried between patients. Other staff members gave out breakfast trays or stacked them onto wheeled carts. People came and went continually.

Mid-morning the doctors came. Jeanmarie watched a group of what appeared to be interns follow an older doctor as he made the rounds of the ward. When they came closer, she thought she heard one of the students address the older man as Dr. Hamilton, the doctor the princess had mentioned. As they came her way her face grew warm. She wondered if he had operated on her and if any of these young interns had been there.

"You're a lucky lass," the big, broad-shouldered doctor leading the group said in a heavy Scottish brogue. He patted Jeanmarie's hand. "Your appendix was as close to bursting as a balloon that canna hold one more breath without exploding. That would have given us a wee bit of trouble, lass." A nurse stood ready to assist while he examined the wound in Jeanmarie's side. "Draining nicely," he announced. Deftly he applied a fresh bandage. Finished, he stepped back. "Looks good. You'll be up and around and as good as new in no time." He smiled and went on to his next patient, followed by his very serious students hurrying to keep up. Jeanmarie hadn't said a word. She wished he had stayed long enough for her to ask about Pearl and the princess and Wilfred. Where were they?

None of the nurses Jeanmarie asked had seen any of the others. The nurse who'd just taken Jeanmarie's temperature said, "All I know is that you were brought down from the recovery room for us to take care of you." She wrote something on the chart at the foot of the bed. "If this war isn't over soon," she added, hanging the chart back in its place, "we'll have to start putting patients to work because we're so short-handed. You say a clown brought you and your friends in? This hospital is bulging with patients, at least two hundred from that circus fire. Sorry, I can't help you out." She pulled the sheets smooth on Jeanmarie's bed and hurried away.

A nagging worry crept into Jeanmarie's heart. Did anyone from the orphanage know she was here? Where was Pearl? And what about Wilfred? He must be somewhere in the place. Why hadn't anyone from the orphanage come? They'd all been sitting in the section to the right of the main entrance in the big top. A terrible thought struck her—what if they hadn't gotten out in time?

Tall, strong Miss Bigler would have done her best to save them. Jeanmarie imagined her trying to lead her charges to safety, smoke and flames all around and above them. She could hear her clear voice telling them all to have courage. Had they made it? A tear slid down Jeanmarie's face as she thought of Winnie, Tess and Maria, little Lizzie, and the others. If only she knew what had happened to them.

By the time Miss Bigler arrived, wearing a prim straw hat on top of her black hair pulled into its usual bun, Jeanmarie had all but given up hope that anyone even knew where she was. She had never seen Miss Bigler looking so mild. "Oh my, you gave us such a fright," Miss Bigler said with a smile as she sat down carefully on the edge of the bed. "Dr. Werner sent me to see you all, and you are my last visit. Thank God all of you are safe. You know about Pearl's trouble, and I suppose you know that Wilfred has a broken arm, some bruises, and some minor burns. They're both doing as well as can be expected."

"But you and the others were so close to the worst part of the fire; how did you get out?" Jeanmarie asked, wiping a tear of relief from her face.

"We were also close to the side flaps, and so we crawled out under the tent flap. My one fear was that you and Pearl would be caught up in the mob before I could go back for you. It was just as I feared, and you had both disappeared into the crowds without a trace. Knowing that I'd lost you two was almost more than I could bear." She patted Jeanmarie's hand. "There were so many people and such chaos that for hours we could find no trace of you. All we could do was pray that God would bring you safely through, and here you are." She smiled again and sat back. "When we did learn where you were you gave us quite a fright over that sudden appendicitis attack."

Jeanmarie didn't enlighten her on how long ago the "sudden attack" had really begun. Miss Bigler went on to explain that Wilfred was in a men's ward in another part of the building and Pearl was in a special ward for people with sight problems. "Just until the doctors know what is going on with her eyes," she said. "It seems that blow on her head may have done some damage to her sight, though that isn't certain. There is also a great deal of swelling around the eyes. With all the soot and debris in the air something might have gotten into her eyes, but there is no obvious damage that the doctors can see. They are not sure exactly what's caused her blindness or if it will heal of itself, but they are hopeful it's temporary." Miss Bigler checked her watch and stood. "Oh, my dear girl, I'm afraid I must leave. It's good to see you looking so bright, and I'm sure you will be up and about in no time."

"I'm so glad you came," Jeanmarie said. Her throat ached for Pearl as she watched Miss Bigler leave in her usual stately manner, black bun sticking out from beneath the hat. It was just like her to see her charges to safety right under the tent side wall instead of heading for the exit. If only they'd all been sitting together Pearl wouldn't be somewhere in the hospital alone and in the dark.

FOUR

A Clown's Suspicions

With the last of her patients tucked in, the night nurse flicked off the light and slipped away. The restless movements of the sick gradually lessened as sleep came. Jeanmarie pulled the sheet up to her chin and burrowed her head deeper into the pillow. A blanket of quiet had settled over the ward full of sleeping patients, but in the bed nearest hers a Spanish girl, about Jeanmarie's age, was definitely awake. Jeanmarie could hear her muffled sobs. The same feeling that rose in her at the sound of anyone or anything in pain pulled at her now, willing her to do something. But what should she do? At supper time she'd heard the kitchen staff, who had not brought a tray for the girl, trying to explain why with gestures. "No eat," the woman had said, shaking her head. "Tomorrow operation, you get it?" The girl had nodded. "That one only speaks Spanish," the woman had said, handing a tray to Jeanmarie.

In the darkness the girl continued to cry softly. Slowly, favoring her bandaged side, Jeanmarie sat up and swung her legs to the floor. Her bare feet made little sound on the cool tiles. Moving carefully she inched her way to the foot of the bed and around to the other side. She bent over, supporting her side, feeling a heaviness and stiffness as if she hadn't walked in a long time. Light from the corridor guided her. In a moment she stood at the girl's bedside, trying to think of the few Spanish words she'd ever heard. "You okay?" she said. It certainly wasn't Spanish, but it was all she could think of at the moment that made sense.

The girl in the bed sniffled and sat up, her face pale in the dim light. A braid of black hair hung down her back. "Okay? No, no." A flood of Spanish followed. Jeanmarie thought she heard the word *operation.* When the girl stopped, Jeanmarie pointed to the ceiling, *"Dios, vaya con Dios."* It was all the Spanish she'd learned from a song they'd sung in music class one time. Once more she tried, this time pointing to the ceiling *"Jesus Cristo,"* and then to her own heart, "loves you," pointing next to the girl and then back at her heart and again to the girl. The girl stared at her. Tears began falling once more, only this time she leaned over and hugged Jeanmarie. *"Gracias, gracias,"* she said. "English you, Español me; *gracias, chiquita."*

Jeanmarie smiled. *"Vaya con Dios,"* she whispered before making her way back to bed. In the morning she walked the long corridor to the washroom. The first door on her right led to the women's room, and beyond it door after door lined a hallway that looked like it went on endlessly. Afraid to try straightening up, she walked slightly bent, keeping one hand against her bandaged stomach. Even short distances seemed long, and twice she stopped to rest against the wall. By the time she reached the ward again, the girl in the bed near her was gone. An aide hummed as she stripped the bed and began washing the metal frame. Jeanmarie stood for a moment to watch.

The aide, a thin woman with a sharp chin and thinning hair, looked up. "You need something?" she asked.

Jeanmarie shook her head. "No thanks. I just wondered what happened to the girl who slept there."

"Can't say. All I know is I got to wash this bed." The aide went on with her cleaning, and Jeanmarie went back to her own bed disappointed. The operation must have been scheduled early. The girl had been so scared. She hoped she was okay.

By noon the girl still hadn't come back. Jeanmarie had just finished the familiar Jell-O, this time served with a bowl of watery soup, when a nurse in a green uniform came to stand by her bed. "You must be the young woman this is for," she said, holding out a small wooden cross on a chain of braided leather. "Your friend, Maria, said you spoke to her last night, and she wanted you to have this. She wore it into the operating room. I'm afraid her heart was very bad." The nurse handed the cross to Jeanmarie.

"But, you can't mean she isn't coming back," Jeanmarie said.

"I'm sorry, but there was nothing anyone could do," the nurse replied. "Before the operation she asked me to take this cross and give it to the girl in the bed next to hers in the ward. She said to tell you *'Vaya con Dios.'* I guess you know that means go with God. It was her way of thanking you. I'm on lunch break, and this is the first chance I've had to bring it to you."

Jeanmarie could hardly speak as she clutched the small cross. "Thank you," she whispered. "But shouldn't this go to her family?"

34

"Poor kid didn't have any family. Seems she wandered in here off the streets. Your friend is surely in a better place, child." The nurse patted Jeanmarie's shoulder and hurried away. Tears ran down as she thought of the lonely, frightened girl of last night. When Jeanmarie had first come to the orphanage, sent there because her own mother and father couldn't care for her, she'd known times of fear and loneliness. In time she'd learned to accept Pearl and the others as a new kind of family that filled in the emptiness, and she couldn't imagine life without them. The girl from the streets had no one. "Only she isn't lonely anymore, God, is she?" Jeanmarie said aloud. She took a deep breath and dried her eyes. Carefully, she slipped the cross around her neck. *"Vaya con Dios."* She would never sing that song again without thinking of the girl.

The ward buzzed with chatter. Jeanmarie lay on her bed watching the visitors who were beginning to arrive in the ward. She could hear some of them speaking what she thought was Spanish and others speaking a language she couldn't identify. She smiled politely at an elderly Chinese gentleman nodding and smiling as he made his way past to the far end of the ward. Bellevue Hospital not only had the biggest ward she'd ever seen, but more kinds of people came to it than she had known lived in the city. Since it was the city's biggest hospital and the only one that took in everyone even if they couldn't pay, the poor of every nationality came.

Fingering the cross on her neck she thought about the Spanish girl and wished she could have said more to her. A heavy feeling of loneliness settled inside her as she listened to families visiting. Some had brought food whose strange spices smelled almost tempting to her. Huddled against the pillows she prepared to be an onlooker when sudden laughter broke out in the ward. Like a wave growing in strength it rippled across the room. She sat up and looked toward the door where the commotion seemed greatest. The tall figure pushing a wheelchair and doing a little dance as he walked was dressed like a clown—Weary Willie! In the wheelchair, wearing a sling on his bandaged arm and a silly grin on his face was Wilfred. Spotting Jeanmarie, Wilfred said something, and the clown pranced his way over to her bedside.

With a grand bow that made the plastic heart on his tattered coat light up, the clown swept his old black hat from his head and said, "Weary Willie at your service, Mademoiselle." Pulling a large white hanky from his pocket, he dusted off the edge of Jeanmarie's bed, polished the rail, put the hanky back in his pocket, and sat down on the edge of Wilfred's wheelchair. Jeanmarie tried not to laugh, because it hurt her stitches, but she could hardly keep from it and quickly put a hand over her side.

"Uh-oh," Weary Willie said. "I've done it now. We plumb forgot about not making you laugh. I do hear laughing may be good for you, but I declare, it would be better if everybody just cried." At this he looked so sad with his black makeup and the large white outlines around his eyes and drooping mouth that Jeanmarie had to press her hand over her mouth not to laugh again.

"Sorry," Jeanmarie said. "I'm really glad to see you. Is the princess okay?"

Willie took off his hat and slicked back his dark hair. "The princess is a hard one to keep down. The doc says he needs to keep her around a while to watch out for infection. He had to stitch up her arm, so a few days' rest will do her good." As he talked, people who'd come over to see him began trickling back to the patients they were visiting, leaving the three of them alone.

"Now, Mademoiselle," Willie said, leaning over confidentially, "we'll let you in on our secret." He tapped Wilfred's shoulder. "This fine young man has two perfectly good legs. We just figured the wheelchair would get us here faster and be a better act." He winked at Jeanmarie.

Wilfred looked at her and laughed. She'd rarely seen Wilfred, the class brain, laugh. "And it worked too," he said. "I guess I ought to stay in it at least until we're back in the hall."

Jeanmarie shook her head and looked at Willie. "Did they find out how the fire happened?" she asked.

Willie scratched his head for a moment. "That's better. Brain's on." He tapped his forehead. "Who started the fire? It wasn't one of us, that's certain. But just who did it? We're not sure." He leaned forward and lowered his voice. "Rumor has it that one of the roustabouts, the circus laborers who put up the tent and that kind of thing, set the fire, but the fire chief's betting it started from a discarded cigarette in the men's room near the main entrance of the tent." Willie sat straight and raised a large, white-gloved hand. "But I'm sure your honors will agree the truly guilty one is the fool who had the big top coated with melted wax and gasoline to waterproof it for the season."

Jeanmarie didn't know if he was serious or still joking. "Wouldn't that mix catch fire easily?" she asked.

"Quicker than you can wink," Willie said. "And the scoundrel responsible is right now waiting to go before a judge along with three others who didn't do their jobs right. They could have helped prevent this whole tragedy." Willie leaned back and closed his eyes for a moment. Opening them he said, "All of us at the circus have been waiting for the next catastrophe to happen. It's an old circus tradition that trouble comes in threes. What with the robbery and fire, who knows what's next?"

"Robbery?" Jeanmarie exclaimed.

"Happened the day of the fire. Someone took the princess's ruby necklace. She always wore it in the spec, the grand parade where all the performers march around the arena. Should have had it with her, but she'd left it in the tent."

"Then it must have been her necklace I saw the man holding, the man in the tent just before you and the princess came. He rushed out when he saw Pearl and me coming," Jeanmarie said.

Willie stood up. "You saw someone?" he asked.

"Yes, one of the laborers—a roustabout, I think, from the way he was dressed—and he limped," she added.

"Dark hair, medium height, left leg slightly shorter than his right?" Willie asked. Jeanmarie nodded. "Slavko," he said. "It has to be him. I warned him once before to stay away from the princess." Willie slapped his thigh with his gloved hand. "Don't say a word to anyone about this. I want to see him first. Now I'll just be going along, your honors. Mind you, return the wheelchair," he called back over his shoulder.

"Whew," Wilfred said. "You never know when he's clowning and when he's not. I'd hate to be Slavko right now."

"But he's a thief, and worse." Scenes from the fire flashed in Jeanmarie's mind. Quickly she shut them out. "If he's responsible for the fire he should be in jail," she said, her voice sounding sharp to her ears.

Wilfred looked thoughtful. "You really shouldn't jump to conclusions," he said. "Maybe he did drop a cigarette in the men's room, and maybe he didn't. And was it an accident or on purpose? You saw somebody with the necklace—that's a fact—and from Willie's description it sounds like that Slavko guy." Wilfred pushed his glasses farther back on his nose. "As to setting the fire, people who set fires deliberately, arsonists you know, aren't usually robbers too." Wilfred looked at

Jeanmarie as if everyone knew these facts. "Arson is a kind of sickness," he went on. "Anyway, why would this Slavko need to set a fire to have time to steal something when the tent was already empty? I mean, the princess was in the ring doing her animal act, wasn't she?"

Jeanmarie pursed her lips. Wilfred's logical mind was like a hard wall she couldn't just run into. He really was the class brain, but even Wilfred couldn't excuse what she'd seen with her own eyes. "Okay. Maybe he did or didn't set the fire, but he's a thief and that's bad enough," she said. "I guess Willie will know what to do about him, and right now it's Pearl I'm worried about."

Wilfred shook his head. "Rotten thing, being blind, you know."

"The doctor said it could be just temporary," Jeanmarie shot back. "Anyway we ought to go see her." Unlike at the orphanage, no one seemed to notice much what patients did most of the day outside of the daily hospital routines, and visiting hours were the freest times of all.

Wilfred looked at the watch on his good arm. "Can't. Visiting hours are about over, and I've still got to get this chair back. We'll have to go tomorrow."

"Right, tomorrow then. I'll meet you here when visiting hours start," Jeanmarie said as Wilfred headed for the door.

She'd meant to ask Miss Bigler the way to Pearl's room, but Wilfred might know. Together they'd find her. Jeanmarie closed her eyes to think about the day they'd seen the roustabout in the princess's tent and frowned.

She didn't hear anyone come until an Irish-sounding voice said cheerfully, "St. Joseph have mercy on us, where's your smilin' face gone, my girl?" The volunteer library cart lady, only without her usual cart, stood smiling at Jeanmarie. "I guess you never expected to be seeing me here on me own time," she said. "But I've a bit of news for you. Your friend, the one you been wearing out the nurses asking about, the poor lass that cannot see, is upstairs, not so far if you don't go getting lost. She's in a wee bit of a room that used to be a closet, on the next floor at the end of the women's ward. What with all the new patients the nurses are after using every corner for beds, but your friend's there all right. Now what do you think of that!"

"I think you are the best, the kindest lady in Bellevue. Thank you, thank you," Jeanmarie said and smiled.

"Well now, and your face is looking more like it ought. I make it me business to do a good thing when I can." The woman's own face grew serious. "I'm not one to go interfering, mind you, but you best be knowing your friend needs a bit of cheering up. What with her eyes all bandaged and them stitches in her head wound she could do with a friend. To say nothing of being by herself in that excuse for a room. The nurses are so shorthanded they've no time for friendly chats. Are you after knowing what I mean?"

"Oh yes," Jeanmarie cried. In her heart she felt a stab of pain for Pearl, alone, not able even to see.

"Well then, love, I'm away to me digs," the woman said. Jeanmarie watched her leave. Visiting hours were over, but she couldn't wait. Tonight after lights-out she'd find Pearl.

Jeanmarie didn't know where the night nurse went at night, but there was no sign of anyone in the darkened hall. She made her way toward the washroom, passed it, and headed down the hall. She didn't dare take the elevator, but when she came to a second one and another farther down the endless hall, she hesitated. The sound of footsteps decided for her, and she slipped inside. The elevator was a small box, dilapidated just like the rest of the building. Cranking and shaking, it took her up to the next floor.

Here too she saw no one in the hallway. She hadn't planned what to do next. On her right a long stretch of wall held door after door, but on the left only one small door stood at the end of an unbroken wall that was probably the women's ward. The door was slightly open. Jeanmarie went to it and looked inside. In the semidarkness, someone on a narrow cot turned and sat up.

"Who's there? Is that the nurse I hear?" The voice was Pearl's.

Twenty minutes later, their hands still clasped together, Pearl said, "I know you have to get back, but promise me you'll come tomorrow as soon as visiting hours start."

Jeanmarie squeezed Pearl's hands. "I will; don't worry."

Pearl's voice dropped to a low tone. "What if I never see you again?" she said.

"Oh, Pearl, don't think like that. The doctor said it might just be a while until your eyes are healed. God will heal you; he has to," Jeanmarie said.

"What if he means for me to be blind, like Fannie Crosby, the hymn writer Miss Bigler told me about? He might, you know. But I want to see so badly. And I'm scared for when they take these bandages off; what if I don't?" she whispered.

"You will, you will," Jeanmarie insisted. She hugged Pearl tightly. "I'll be back tomorrow," she promised.

FIVE

"Air Raid"

Wilfred was nowhere in sight. Visiting hours had started nearly fifteen minutes ago. Maybe he'd forgotten or Willie had stopped by again. Jeanmarie didn't expect any visitors. Her own mother never even visited the orphanage. In the beginning her father had come, and each painful visit they'd sat like strangers not knowing what to say to each other. When the visits grew fewer she'd felt relief. The orphanage was her real home now. She looked at the clock on the wall for the second time and then across the ward. Wilfred still hadn't come, and she couldn't wait any longer.

Pearl was seated on a chair by her bed, waiting. "I thought you weren't coming," she wailed. Jeanmarie hurried to sit on the edge of the bed across from her and clasped her hands. "Wilfred was supposed to meet me and come too, but I guess he couldn't. Anyway, I'm here, and I thought we could walk down the hall together, if you like."

"Anywhere, so long as it's out of this room. I've felt my way clear around it, and I don't believe it's any bigger than a good-size closet," Pearl said. Jeanmarie smiled. She wouldn't tell Pearl that it *was* a closet, not yet.

Jeanmarie walked slowly, letting Pearl hold on to her arm. At least she could walk better today instead of being bent over and feeling like her side weighed a ton, though it still felt sore and swollen. There was so much to talk about, and Pearl, free of her small room, wanted to know about everything. They'd hardly gotten back to the room when the bell signaling the end of visiting hours sounded. "I'll be here tomorrow," Jeanmarie promised, settling Pearl back in her chair. A sudden pain in her side made her draw in her breath sharply.

"We didn't walk too much for you, did we?" Pearl asked anxiously.

Jeanmarie put a hand against her side. "It's just muscles trying to heal back together. It comes and goes, sort of like a catch in the side when you run too long. Well, I'll see you later."

In the hallway Jeanmarie made her way to the elevator. "Nothing like a little help," she whispered, stepping inside it.

She pushed the button and waited. Then on its own the elevator went up instead of down, screeching to a stop at the next floor. The door opened and a woman pushed her way in hollering, "Air raid! Air raid! Have to get to the bomb shelter!" She quickly pressed the bottom elevator button. The woman grinned, showing two missing teeth.

Jeanmarie stepped back against the elevator wall. "You mean there's an air-raid drill?" she said. "I didn't hear the sirens."

43

"It's an air raid alright. Lucky if we make it to the shelter on time."

Jeanmarie stared at her, noticing for the first time the woman's odd outfit. She wore a skirt and blouse and in spite of the heat had wrapped a wool shawl around her shoulders, but instead of shoes, she was wearing hospital slippers. Her short brown hair was uncombed.

The elevator stopped, and the woman grabbed Jeanmarie's arm and pulled her along into what looked like a basement full of storage rooms. The hallway ran on farther than Jeanmarie could see. Small lights on the walls lit the corridor enough for her to know there was no one else in sight. What was going on? Before she could think, the woman began calling loudly.

"Air raid! Air raid!" the woman yelled, looking around her. "Where is everybody?" she asked with a confused look on her face, her dark eyes troubled.

A shiver went through Jeanmarie, and her stomach lurched. Something was wrong about all this. Every instinct told her she needed to get out of there. "I think we have the wrong floor," she suggested. "We better go back upstairs and find the others," she added hopefully.

"No, no," the woman insisted. "The shelter is probably down that way." She pointed to the long corridor of doorways, most of them without doors. "Hurry up!" she shouted. "I can hear those bombs coming."

Jeanmarie felt her stomach sink. She heard nothing. Ahead of her the woman peered into room after room. She wanted to turn and run. Should she leave her and go for help?

Before she could choose, the woman turned around, an anxious look on her face. "We should have listened to the air-raid warden. They've moved the shelter. We'll have to go back up."

44

"You're right," Jeanmarie said. Quickly she pressed the elevator button. Her legs felt like rubber, and goose bumps ran down her arms. At least they were going back up out of the basement.

When the elevator came, the woman flung open the door and pushed past Jeanmarie. "Get in, get in," she urged.

"Coming," Jeanmarie said. As she stepped into the elevator something made her look down the long corridor. At the far end just before it turned a corner, she saw a figure running, a man limping as he ran. The roustabout! Even in the dim light she felt sure it had to be him.

From the elevator the woman screeched, "Air raid! We have to hurry! Get in, get in!" Jeanmarie swallowed hard and stepped inside the elevator. The woman pressed all of the buttons, then pressed each one again. For a few seconds the elevator sat motionless. Jeanmarie's heart beat fast, and she prayed silently for the thing to work. With a lurch and a noisy grinding the elevator began climbing, only it didn't stop at Jeanmarie's floor or the next one. When it came to a jerking, grinding halt she pushed open the door, ready to get off no matter where they were. The woman followed her yelling, "Air raid! Air raid!"

A nurse came running toward them. "Why, Nellie, the air raid is all over, dear. Let me get someone to take you back. Your supper will be waiting and everyone is looking for you." One of the staff had already come with a wheelchair, and Nellie took her seat in it as if she had done this before. As Nellie was wheeled away the nurse turned to Jeanmarie. "Did she frighten you much? She does this at least once a month, poor thing, but she's harmless. Nobody has figured out exactly how she manages to get out." Gently the nurse patted Jeanmarie's arm. "From the looks of you I'd say you needed a ride yourself. Aren't you the young lady with the

45

bad appendix? I was on duty in the emergency room when they brought you in. Looks like they did a good job, and I'm sure you're feeling a lot better now. Why don't I get someone to wheel you back to your ward?"

"I'm really fine," Jeanmarie said. "For a little while I thought maybe there was an air raid when Nellie came running onto the elevator just as I was going to get out. We ended up in the basement, I think, before she changed her mind and came up here."

One of the aides popped her head outside the ward and called, "Nurse, we need you in here!"

The nurse sighed. "We're so short-staffed thanks to this war; I have to run. If you're sure you're alright I'll be off. Otherwise you can wait here a bit, and I'll be back. Coming!" she called, hurrying away to the ward.

Jeanmarie looked at the elevator, gingerly pushed the down button, and waited. This time it worked, groaning as usual but stopping at her floor. She breathed a sigh of relief but nearly choked when the door opened to reveal Wilfred standing in front of her.

"Didn't expect you," he said, surprise on his face. "I just came by to tell you I couldn't make it during visiting hours, but you weren't there. Had to get a treatment for the burns on my back, and it took the whole time," he explained.

"Oh," Jeanmarie said. She hadn't known about Wilfred's back burns. "Well, it's okay; I saw Pearl. And you'll never guess what else I saw." Quickly she filled him in on Nellie and the roustabout. "It had to be him, I know it was," she said.

"What is he doing down in the old basement?" Wilfred asked, pushing his glasses back on his nose.

"Hiding from the law, of course," Jeanmarie stated. "What better place? I didn't see a lot of it, but you can tell from the stone walls and the old stuff around that the place is ancient. I bet nobody ever goes down there."

Wilfred looked thoughtful. "I'd sure like to see that," he said. "The oldest parts of Bellevue were built back in the nineteenth century, and they just kept building onto it, I guess." He pushed his glasses back on his nose. "I read a book about it. And though it's no longer used, somewhere in the old part is an old chapel." His eyes were bright and his voice excited. "Maybe we ought to take a look down there."

Jeanmarie tried not to smile. She wanted to go back to the basement but not alone. "Well, if you're sure. But what if we run right into that fellow?"

Wilfred's glasses slid down slightly as he looked at her. "You said he ran away from you, didn't you? He's probably already gone now that he knows someone might have seen him. And if he is still down there, he's going to be more careful about being seen. If someone did want to hide down there, he could find plenty of places, at least until he ran out of food. From what I've read there are old passageways besides the tunnel running under the buildings, and there are exits all over the place. Even upstairs the place is so huge student doctors get lost all the time." Wilfred stepped into the elevator. "I doubt we'll see the fellow again."

Jeanmarie nodded. "We'll have to take Pearl too. I promised her I'd visit. If you could borrow that wheelchair again she can ride in it."

"Right, good idea. We can tell her what the old chapel looks like once we find it." From the pocket of his hospital robe Wilfred drew out a small booklet and, holding it in his good arm, began reading as the elevator door closed.

"I'll count on it," Jeanmarie called. But she knew he'd come. The idea of seeing the old chapel had him hooked. Wilfred couldn't resist learning about things like that. Just maybe they'd find some kind of clue to prove the roustabout had been there, otherwise she'd be content never to see the basement again. Only she had seen him. Had he seen her? She stood still as a thought struck her. Of course he'd heard Nellie crying "Air raid" at the top of her lungs, unless the man was stone deaf. They'd have to be careful this time. Pressing a hand to her side she walked slowly back to the ward.

SIX

Footsteps in the Hall

Pearl sat propped against her pillow. Between her fingers and fork she'd picked up something that felt squishy. When she finally managed to bring it to her mouth, she recognized the bland taste of carrots. Feeling with her fingers Pearl found the round meatballs the nurse had told her were there and lifted one. It tasted a little like meat mixed heavily with bread crumbs. Somehow the next one rolled off the plate, and though she felt everywhere on her tray she couldn't find it. There were no others; still hungry, she felt for the small dish of Jell-O. Some of it she got into her mouth; the rest slid from the spoon or refused to go on the spoon at all. Why did they have to serve Jell-O?

Angrily Pearl tossed her spoon down and reached for the roll that had been next to her plate. Only it wasn't there. She gave up searching and wiped her hands on the napkin the nurse had tucked under her chin. With a yank she took it off and tossed it down in front of her. The sound of the trays clanging onto the wheeled cart caught her attention. She waited tensely for it to stop at her room. Would she know by the sound when it did? Instead she heard footsteps coming toward her.

"Finished, are you?" a voice asked. Pearl nodded and gritted her teeth. At this rate she'd starve to death. "Good. Then I'll be off with your tray." In a moment the footsteps sounded again and Pearl listened hard to hear all she could. How easy life had been when she could see. A light knock caught her attention. "Who's there?" she asked.

"A friend who came to the hospital with you in the car," the voice said. "It's me—Princess. I thought you might know me by my circus name. Maybe you saw me in the ring with the cats just before the fire broke out?"

"Oh yes. I remember you," Pearl cried. "You were with the black leopards in the cage. And it was your tent we were in just before you and Weary Willie brought Jeanmarie and Wilfred and me here. Willie was the one who found us by the animal cages. I guess you know. But you were hurt too, weren't you?"

"Yes, child, but not so much. May I sit down by you?" she asked.

"Please do," Pearl said. "Can you stay a little while? The evenings are so long. Nobody comes until bedtime once the trays are picked up."

"Yes, so it is for me too. I decided I needed to have some company tonight, and here I am." As the princess sat down something fell to the floor, a roll. It landed next to a meatball already there. She shook her head, her face brightening as she opened the box in her hand. "I hope you like chocolate candy," she said. "Dear Willie brought me such a large box I must share them. This one is creme-filled; will that do to start with?" Carefully she closed Pearl's fingers around the candy.

"Delicious," Pearl said, savoring the sweet, creamy taste. "Thanks so much. I think I missed some of my supper. Guess I'm still learning to feed myself now that I have to wear these bandages on my eyes."

Princess took Pearl's hand and placed another chocolate in it. "This one has a cherry center, one of my favorites." She took Pearl's other hand in hers. "You know, child, practice and determination are what it takes to do anything. I'm hoping you will soon see again, but in the meantime if you are willing to learn to do without your eyes, you will get by."

Pearl felt a choking sob in her throat. "I feel so clumsy, and I can't do anything right. It's so awful," she wailed.

Princess took her in her arms and rocked her like a little child. "Once I felt like you do now. After my mother and my father died."

Pearl raised her head and wiped at her face with her hands. "You're an orphan too?" she said.

"Yes," Princess replied. "I was born in Czechoslovakia. My parents were circus performers too. They taught me everything I know about the wild cats. But one day fever struck our village, and I lost them both. For weeks after that I could not do anything right. My performances suffered, and I almost gave up." She handed Pearl another chocolate.

"What happened then?" Pearl asked.

"Our little circus needed to travel on, and I decided not to go with it, but thanks to an old friend of my father's, a very fine high-wire artist, I changed my mind. A few years before, our friend's brother had fallen from the high wire and died, and for a little while my friend could not perform well. Not even the simple things he had always done before were easy. 'The only way to find your way back is to thank God for the gifts he has given you and trust him with the things you cannot understand,' he told me that day. 'We show our thankfulness to him when we use our gifts well,' he said, 'because our bodies and our minds are his works of art.'"

Princess paused a moment. "He was right," she said. "Do you know we can learn to listen, feel, hear with our whole body? For my friend, when he walked on the high wire, his feet became eyes and ears too." She patted Pearl's arm. "With the cats I must notice everything, ears to tail, and when my back is turned, every sound becomes a signal. Scratches and misses are part of the learning, but practice and more practice produce the good results. You have the gift of a fine body, and it will learn for you, I know. My friend was right, child, a trusting, thankful heart frees you to heal."

"I'll try," Pearl said. She wanted to ask the questions that crowded in on her, big ones, hard ones, but she didn't. Wishing she could see, she asked instead, "And what about your arm? I saw when the leopard struck you in the cage. May I call you Princess?"

"Yes, of course, and I remember that your name is Pearl." Princess's voice had a slight accent that sounded foreign to Pearl but was one she liked. "My poor cats could smell the fire, and so I do not blame them for their actions. One must never forget that the leopard is not like the tiger or the lion or even the jaguar. Each kind of wild cat has its own temperament, and a good trainer knows that leopards are always dangerous and require great care even for the best of trainers. And though I love working with the cats, I have great respect for them. Because of the fire there was little time to act, and Nana, the wise one, strikes like lightning if she is pushed too far too fast. So, I have a few stitches and a good number of deep scratches, but nothing serious if we avoid infection."

"I thought you were the bravest person I'd ever seen," Pearl said.

Princess laughed. "Right now I'm glad to be here in the hospital for a few days. If you promise not to tell I will let you in on a little secret."

"My lips are sealed," Pearl said.

"Well, it's this," Princess continued. "Anyone who is around a circus long will sometimes get rashes from the animals, especially from the elephants, though monkeys and cats too can cause it. Unfortunately I have such a rash, and it is quite noticeable. Simply put, I am far too vain and want to hide for a while until it goes away. So now you know my secret: vanity."

Pearl knew she was smiling. "Your secret is safe," she said. "I can only remember you as beautiful."

"Why, thank you," Princess said softly. "I try like all of the performers to dress as brightly as possible for our audience. I often wear the necklace that was my mother's. It was not expensive, only colored glass, but beautifully set in the chain." Her voice seemed to be sad. "I can't understand why anyone would steal it, but it's gone, and I guess I will never see it again."

"I'm sorry," Pearl said, meaning it. "You must feel terrible losing something that belonged to your mother."

"Yes, I do; someone stole the necklace from my trunk. I had left it there instead of wearing it that day. Even my gold-framed picture was gone. Who would do such a thing? Ah, well, not everyone is as good as my Emil. That is Willie's real name, and mine is Maya." She stood up. "I must obey the good doctor and go back to my bed now. May I leave some of these chocolates with you?"

"Thanks," Pearl said, holding out her hands. "I probably ought to store them under my pillow." She laughed and took the box Princess laid in her hands.

"Remember—trust, practice, and determination, and more practice," Princess said. "Good night; sleep well." She bent and gently kissed Pearl's forehead.

Pearl sighed and listened carefully to the sound of the princess's footsteps until she could no longer hear them. Opening the box she discovered that it was more than half full of candy. The box was too big to put under her pillow, but she didn't want to lose it somewhere off the bed or the chair either. "Think," she told herself, trying to imagine what her bed looked like with its neatly tucked-in sheets. The nurses were always smoothing the sheet that covered her at night and tucking it in at the sides. Reaching below her feet under the sheet she felt around. It was tight at both sides, just the place. She slid the box under the sheet to the bottom of the bed and, satisfied, turned on her side to sleep.

Back in her own small room the princess had gone straight to bed. The room, though small, was a private one. Each year the circus gave free performances at Bellevue, and in return the staff gave the sick or hurt performers special care, which included the private room whenever possible. To reach the room from the main part of the old hospital one had to go through a long tunnel, and the walk had tired the princess. Her long, golden hair lay spread out on the pillow, her face rosy from the heat or perhaps a touch of fever, and she slept deeply.

No one saw the figure with a limp hurrying toward the princess's room. At this time of night except for the emergency room, most of the vast hospital quieted down. The war had taken away many of the staff, and there were never enough doctors or nurses even during the day. At night the staff became a small crew, and many of them, overworked and exhausted, tried to catch some sleep while patients slept. Silence lay over the new administration building and in the tunnel connecting it to the rest of the hospital.

Near the tunnel the new chapel, its lights turned down for the night, remained open as usual. Tonight a latecomer sought refuge there. The man, dressed in a white shirt and dark pants, limped as he made his way to the altar. From the large bouquet of flowers placed beside the altar he pulled out a handful of pink and white snapdragons, added two roses, and wrapped the whole with a circle of large, lacy ferns. Holding the flowers, he left, taking the tunnel to the main hospital. Again no one seemed to be around as he made his way to the room familiar to many of the circus people who had used it themselves or had visited fellow employees there.

In the dimly lit hallway of this wing there were no wards, only various labs and other such rooms. The man's limping steps echoed softly, and now and then he glanced nervously behind him. No one came. At last he reached his goal.

For several minutes he stood at the doorway of the familiar room until his eyes, adjusting to the dimness, made out the sleeping Princess. Inch by inch he crept toward her bed, each step noiseless. At the bedside he stood silently for a minute, then gently laid the flowers on the night table next to the bed. Carefully, like a shadow, he glided to the door and out into the hallway. A few minutes' walk brought him to an elevator. He slipped inside.

Princess slept soundly, dreaming of her big cats and scolding Nana firmly. In the warm July air the smell of the flowers close to her head gave off a heavy sweetness, and she smiled in her sleep.

SEVEN

Secret Passageways

Jeanmarie tied her hospital robe tighter and walked past a group of visitors into the corridor to wait for Wilfred. Like many of the orphans at Apple Valley, both his parents were dead. In some odd way she had come to count on Wilfred's steadiness, almost like the brother she'd never had. Practical, scientific Wilfred wasn't at all like her, but he always seemed to be there when she needed another brain, and more, she knew he understood her. She had counted on his help more than once.

She smiled as she saw him coming from the elevator, pushing an ancient wheelchair in front of him with his good arm. "Thought nobody would miss this old thing. The wheels turn and the brakes work, so I guess it will do," he said.

Jeanmarie rubbed her hand against the old wood of the high-backed chair. "If Pearl could only see this, she'd have a story to go with it in no time," she said. "You know how she loves books, not your scientific kind but good stories."

Wilfred held open the elevator door. "She may not like scientific books, but she can pitch a ball better than anybody in the orphanage, including most of the fellows." He shook his head. "I hope the doctor's right about her eyes healing again."

When they reached Pearl's room she was sitting in the chair at her bedside, waiting for them. "Have we got news," Jeanmarie said, plopping herself on the edge of Pearl's bed. "We've seen the roustabout, the circus laborer, the one we caught in Princess's tent just after the fire. We think it's Slavko; at least that's what Willie thinks."

"Hold on," Wilfred interrupted. "I didn't see him; you did."

"Well, I *did* see him; I'm sure of that," Jeanmarie stated. "And you won't believe where." Quickly she filled in the details for Pearl.

Pearl put her hand over her mouth. "If he's the thief who stole the princess's necklace and gold-framed picture, we ought to tell her right away."

Puzzled, Jeanmarie said, "What picture? I saw a necklace in Slavko's hand that day in the tent, but I don't know anything about the picture. How do you know about it?"

"The princess came to see me last night," Pearl explained. "She told me about her missing necklace and the picture. The necklace belonged to her mother. We've got to tell her about this!"

"Hold on a minute," Wilfred said. "Even if you tell the princess you saw Slavko, or whoever it was you saw, he's probably gone by now. And you don't know for certain it was Slavko." He pushed his glasses higher on his nose. "We ought to take a look around first where you spotted him. See if we find any evidence. The old chapel is down there somewhere too. We might as well take a look at it, as long as we're down there anyway." His voice sounded matter-of-fact, but Jeanmarie knew nothing would keep him from finding that chapel.

"I say we tell the princess first," Pearl insisted, "though I don't know where her room is exactly. She did say she came through the tunnel from her room into this part of the hospital to visit me. And I know her real first name is Maya. That should help."

"Did you know this place is so big even the interns get lost in it?" Wilfred said. "We'd have to ask where she is over in the administration building, which happens to be connected to this part of the hospital by a tunnel. But I think you need her full name to find her. Thousands of patients come here every year."

Jeanmarie raised her eyebrows. "But how many princesses?" Wilfred sounded just like Wilfred, his head always full of facts he seemed to acquire wherever he went.

"Wilfred is right," Pearl said. "In the circus everyone calls her Princess, but whoever keeps the lists of patients would have to put down her real name—Maya something."

"I guess so," Jeanmarie said, "but even if we can't find her that way I'm sure on the other side of the tunnel someone will know who we're talking about. Everyone knows about the circus fire, and how many tunnels can there be?"

"Maybe only one long one, but what about all the passages leading out of it?" Wilfred noted.

"Well, maybe they're labeled, and we can tell something that way. We need to decide. It's already getting late, and visiting hours will be over before we're through." Jeanmarie had no watch, but she knew they'd already wasted enough time. "If we go down there we can look around where I saw Slavko, then find the tunnel and try to find the princess." She saw the question in Wilfred's eyes. "And if we spot the old chapel along the way we could take a quick look at it too," she added. "Okay?" Wilfred nodded. How they would fit all that into the visiting hours she wasn't sure.

"I guess if that's what you think we should do, it's okay with me," Pearl said. "Lead on; literally that is," she added in a barely audible voice.

With Pearl in the wheelchair, Wilfred pushing, and Jeanmarie walking alongside, they drew a few stares from staff hurrying by in the hallway, but no one stopped to question them.

The elevator didn't come when Jeanmarie pushed the button. She waited and tried again. It still didn't work. "Now what do we do? We can't take the stairs," she said, giving the wooden door a thump.

"Try another one," Wilfred said. "They won't all be busy." He pushed the old chair along at a faster pace. Determined to keep up, Jeanmarie pressed a hand against her side and hurried. The corridor turned before they came to another elevator. The three entered it quickly. Inside the dingy box Jeanmarie pushed the bottom button. It worked. But when the door opened to let them out they were at a part of the basement Jeanmarie didn't recognize. On the right the corridor ran past what looked like more storage rooms, and on the left it curved. "Let's try going left," she suggested. Maybe around the curve she'd see the elevator she and Nellie had taken. A slight shiver ran down her back. Anyone could be hiding somewhere down here. The place was huge.

Seated in the chair Pearl moved her head from side to side. "It smells damp here," she said. "Do you see the tunnel?"

"Not yet," Jeanmarie answered. Luckily Pearl couldn't see the giant cobwebs hanging in corners, or the cracked walls.

The whole place looked like no one ever came here, but then why did the elevator stop here? And where was the one they were looking for?

"Will you take a look at that," Wilfred said and whistled. He stood by the wall running his hand over some large yellow stones. "This yellow stone is really ancient," he explained to Pearl. "You can tell that it's different from the newer gray stone. It even feels older. We must be in the oldest part of the hospital before they built on to it. The old chapel could be near here!" Wilfred sounded excited.

Pearl drew her arms in close to herself. "I guess that means spiders and things live here too. Do you see the other elevator yet?"

"Nope," Wilfred said. "But don't worry about anything living down here. Most of the animal and insect kingdom stay out of people's way."

"They're not the ones I worry about. It's the few who don't," Pearl said.

"Wilfred's right, I'm sure," Jeanmarie soothed. "You know how even the mice back at the orphanage are pretty shy." Jeanmarie didn't mind things like mice. Snakes and spiders she could do without. "Anyway, we can't be far from the tunnel." Weren't tunnels always underground? This place was certainly below ground. "It has to be down here," she said. She didn't dare say what she was thinking, but the shadows in the rooms they passed and the quiet were beginning to play tricks on her imagination. Anyone, anything could be in one of them and who would ever know? After a series of turns the main corridor split. Now which way?

"Why don't you two stay put," Wilfred suggested, "and I'll run on down that left fork and see if I spot another elevator."

"Oh please," Pearl begged, "don't you dare leave me here alone. Jeanmarie, where are you?"

"Here; I'm right here," Jeanmarie said, taking Pearl's hand. "Wilfred can go ahead and see what's there. I need a rest anyway." She sat against the arm of the wheelchair, still holding Pearl's hand. "Mostly, from what I see, it's just old storage rooms down here. I guess the hospital keeps all the stuff they don't need anymore just in case they might want it someday," she said.

"I know it sounds strange," Pearl said, "but in the dark I can imagine all kinds of things I know I wouldn't think of if I could see."

Jeanmarie closed her own eyes, trying to feel how it would be but opened them quickly. Even the dimness was better than the dark. She squeezed Pearl's hand.

"Determination, that's what I need," Pearl said in a low voice, "and practice. Princess told me that." Turning her bandaged face toward Jeanmarie she said, "Did you know it takes determination to trust? It's hard to do, but it's the same as training the big cats, and it takes practice."

"Don't worry," Jeanmarie said. "I won't leave you." Pearl couldn't see the tear that Jeanmarie wiped away from her own face. God would surely heal Pearl, and trust was just what they both needed. "Good for Princess," she said. "That makes three of us determined that you'll see again."

"I want to believe it," Pearl said, "but I didn't mean trust that way. The princess said when things happen that we don't understand, you know, bad things, we need to choose to trust God and thank him for the gifts we still have. It's something I have to try. Like learning to use my ears and my hands while I can't see, sort of like seeing with my whole body. If I practice hard I can learn, and I want to, but I don't think I can do it alone, not yet."

Just then Wilfred came hurrying back. "I can't believe I've found it!" he said breathlessly.

"The elevator? Where?" Jeanmarie asked.

"No, no, the chapel," Wilfred said. "Wait till you see it. What a find."

Jeanmarie groaned. "Then you didn't find the tunnel that way either? We need to try the other way."

"Well, you can see how the hall goes on and on, and there's still the other fork," Wilfred explained. "A tunnel is supposed to be a kind of shortcut connection usually, so it could be anywhere. And remember, there could be more than one. But you have to take a look at this place," Wilfred insisted. "It's history right before your eyes just the way it looked years ago. The old fixtures and all, even the railing and wood carvings are there." Wilfred's eyes shone. "You can take Pearl with you and go look while I run down the other fork and check for your elevator and the tunnel. It will only take a few minutes, and you're not likely to see anything like it again. Go straight ahead and you'll come to it. You can't miss the carved doorway."

"I wish I could see it," Pearl said. "It's probably just like something in a Dickens novel. You ought to have a look," she urged Jeanmarie. "You can be my eyes too, while Wilfred's gone."

Jeanmarie touched Pearl's shoulder lightly. "We can take a look, but I think you better walk behind the chair. I guess I shouldn't be pushing anything yet." Her side felt heavy, and she had no idea how strong the stitches holding her wound together were.

"Oh, Jeanmarie, I can't believe I forgot about your operation. You sound so healthy and okay, and here I am riding because I can't see where to go. I should be wheeling you."

Jeanmarie laughed. "Save your energy. Besides, I'm fine, just don't want to break these stitches." Pearl stood and let Jeanmarie guide her to the back of the chair and place her hands on the handlebars. "I can steer when we need it," Jeanmarie said, grasping one of the chair handles below Pearl's hand.

"I'll be back," Wilfred sang out cheerfully as he turned down the right fork.

"Straight ahead," Jeanmarie ordered. The dampness of the corridor felt cool, better than the hot July air upstairs. But in spite of the high slits of windows in the stone walls of the rooms they passed and the small lights in the corridor, an eeriness lay over the place. Jeanmarie wondered how it would be down here at night. The silence seemed ominous, and she found herself glancing around as if something or someone might suddenly appear. In another few moments they came to a wide, carved wooden door held open by a length of chain fastened to the wall. It was just as Wilfred said; they'd found the chapel. "Oh, Pearl, you ought to see this!" she cried. "The chapel is beautiful, and you were right, it's just like in a Dickens story."

Reverence in her voice, Pearl whispered, "Tell me what you see."

Looking around, Jeanmarie described the chapel, trying not to leave out anything. "That's it," she finished. She hadn't mentioned the layers of dust and cobwebs thick in the small room, not wanting to spoil the picture for Pearl. "It's something," she said, and it was. The little chapel still had a feeling of peace about it. She could almost picture patients coming to pray here. A sense of timelessness stole over her, and she stifled a yawn. "Wilfred ought to be back by now," she said. "Unless he's discovered another chapel or something." She laughed.

"Sounds like Wilfred," Pearl said. "But maybe he went all the way through the tunnel to find the princess on his own. You know Wilfred. He might have decided it would be a waste of time to come back for us and then go through the tunnel again, especially if it's a long one."

Jeanmarie tucked a loose strand of hair behind her ear. "I suppose, being Wilfred, he'd think the whole thing through. But if he doesn't come soon visiting hours will be over, and we'll be missing persons or something." They'd never have time to look for evidence that Slavko had been down here, if Wilfred didn't hurry. She and Pearl should have gone with him.

"Maybe we can walk around the chapel, and I can get an idea of how big it is," Pearl said. With Jeanmarie helping, they walked completely around the chapel, stopping to feel the wooden rail at the front, the carved decorations, the candlesticks, and the pews.

"The stained glass windows above the altar look like blue and gold angels with white wings spread," Jeanmarie said. Even though they were darkened with dust she knew they'd been beautiful once. "Well, we're back to where we started, and I can't believe Wilfred still isn't here." She ought to do something, but what?

"It feels so peaceful," Pearl said in a low voice. "Let's sit in one of the pews while we wait. Think of all the people who came here."

Jeanmarie wanted to do anything but sit. She looked at Pearl and sighed. She ought to be glad one of them wasn't worried. "Might as well," she said. "With your imagination you'll probably be a famous writer," she added as Pearl felt her way into the pew. Jeanmarie had let go of Pearl's arm and turned to glance once more toward the doorway in hope of seeing Wilfred. Instead she gasped as a man ran past, a man with a limp—Slavko!

"What is it? Are you hurting?" Pearl cried.

"No, not me," she whispered. "I think I just saw that man, Slavko, running past the door. I don't think he saw us." She raised her voice. "He has a limp, and I'm certain it was him." Jeanmarie clutched Pearl's arm. "Can you sit here a minute while I look? He's probably out of sight already, but maybe I can spot him."

"Go. Only hurry right back," Pearl pleaded.

Jeanmarie rushed to the doorway. Far down the corridor where it turned, a flash of white disappeared around the corner. Slavko! There was no sign of Wilfred, but he should be back any moment with the princess. The idea of help on the way pushed her on. "He won't get away this time," she thought, hurrying down the hall. He'd turned the corner, but she might still be able to spot him.

EIGHT

Trapped!

Wilfred groaned. The crashing all around him had stopped. He opened his eyes and shut them again. The air seemed full of dust. He could taste dirt in his mouth. One minute he'd been on the old creaking stairway, and the next the whole thing had collapsed. He opened his eyes again. He'd fallen and lay flat on his back. In the dim light above him half the dirt wall seemed to have come away with the stairs. A dark cavelike hole gaped where the wall had been. Dazed, he remembered following a tunnel to a large room and then starting down the stairway. He tried to move and cried out as pain shot through him. A terrible weight pressed against him, holding him pinned down.

His broken left arm throbbed inside its cast and sling. He tried moving again. Like lightning, pain

67

flashed through his shoulder down where he thought his ribs should be. Wilfred bit his lips till the pain quieted some. He hadn't really moved, but the effort to try had caused terrible pain. His head seemed free and inching it sideways he blinked and stared dumbfounded. Where his good arm and shoulder should have been was a mound of dirt and stone. Flat on his back, unable to move, he couldn't even use the fingers of the free arm in the cast to dig himself out. The sling, twisted under him, held the cast tight against his chest, and he was sure he'd done something to his shoulder and possibly his ribs on that side. He closed his eyes to think.

He tried to swallow, but his throat felt dry. Once more he tried to move. This time he heard a scream as a whirl of colored stars flashed before his eyes. When the pain ebbed he whispered, "No use." He couldn't free himself. The only thing left was to shout for help until someone came. He rested, then called out, "Help, someone; down here! Help, somebody!"

He waited for several minutes then called again. How long he kept up his efforts—rest, shout, rest, call—he didn't know, but his head ached and the buried half of his body seemed horribly cold and dead as long as he didn't move it. His other side and the arm in the cast hurt fiercely. He knew his voice was weakening, growing hoarser each time he called.

Feebly, he tried again. This time as he peered up in the dim light to the gaping hole where the stairs had been, a white face stared at him then suddenly disappeared. Someone had seen him!

Hope surged through Wilfred. "Help me!" he cried. "I can't move!" Silence followed his cry. "Must have gone off for help," Wilfred comforted himself. "The fellow could have called down a word like 'hang on, I'm coming,' but at least he's no time-waster—went straight off for help." Worn out by pain Wilfred felt his eyes closing and fought to keep them open. All he needed to do now was wait for the rescue crew. And one thing more: "Thank you, God," he whispered.

Huddled in a corner against the wall, well away from the collapsed stair, the young man Wilfred had seen wore a look of anguish on his face. The man moaned softly. "If I don't go for help, the boy will die. But what can I do? How can I explain being down here? By now the police are looking for me. They'll recognize me and might even blame me for the boy's accident." He fell to his knees, covered his face, and prayed. "O God, what should I do? I never meant to hurt anyone." A sob escaped his throat. "I'll be blamed for the fire. You know I can't go for help." He wept, then grew still. "What can I do?" He stood to his feet and looked wildly about in the dim light. No rope, no ladder, nothing. In one of the storage rooms he had seen old stuff left by workmen from some long-ago job. Maybe he'd find a ladder, something he could use to reach the boy. He'd need some kind of shovel too. He ran back into the main corridor, limping as he went.

Like a sixth sense he knew exactly where he was and what turns to take; once he saw a path he never forgot it. As a guide in his own country he had been one of the best. Already he knew the old corridor with its turns and tunnels as if it were a mountain path or a forest trail. There by the broken yellow patch of stone near the bottom of the wall was another abandoned tunnel, a short one leading back to the storage room he wanted near the little church room.

He hurried through the tunnel back to the corridor and came out near the storage rooms. He was about to enter the one where he'd seen discarded workmen's tools, when the sound of voices startled him.

Tense with fear he stood undecided. If he was discovered they would demand explanations or bring the police down after him. He had moved his hiding place once already, deeper into the old part of the building, confident that no one came there anymore. But someone was here. Trembling he pressed a hand against his chest. Beneath his hand he felt the emptiness of his shirt pocket and hastily searched it. The necklace—he must have left it in his hiding place with the picture! He couldn't let anyone find them. He stood for a second, thinking what to do. To reach his hiding place he must go past the church room where the voices came from. He must run like a shadow, his soft-soled shoes making no sound, and be out of sight before anyone could follow. If he was careful whoever was in the church might not even notice. Whatever the risk, he must first get to the necklace and the picture, then he would think about the boy.

To anyone watching, he ran strangely with a kind of hopping gait. But his limp no longer bothered him, and except for the fact that one leg was shorter than the other, his muscles were strong from hard work. He had learned to run fast in spite of his limp.

Where the corridor turned he disappeared into the first storage room, a large one with a small chamber cut into the outside wall. An air of dampness and ancient stone smelling of earth filled both rooms. Two narrow slits high on the stone wall let in a little light. In the smaller room the window had been shuttered over and nailed fast. Slavko had already loosened one corner of it. One good yank and the whole thing would come undone giving him a quick escape route to the outside. He was certain no one came here, but if they did, the shadowy inner room would help to hide him.

In a corner of the small room hidden from the doorway he had set a discarded pail upside down. On its top lay the necklace and the picture. Slavko picked them up and took them into the larger room. Except for a few discarded odds and ends of rusted pipes and an old rusted iron bed there was nothing in the large room that might be of use to anyone, and here he had felt safe. Sitting on the edge of the old bed frame he held the necklace up. Even in the dim light it sparkled as it swayed in his hand. On his lap lay the princess's picture. A sob broke from his throat. He could never go back to his old job, never see her again. He did not hear the cautious footsteps approach the room and stop in the doorway.

NINE

Face-to-Face with the Enemy

Jeanmarie slowed to a halt as she turned the corner where Slavko had disappeared and stared at the empty corridor ahead. She'd lost him and might as well go back. At that moment a slight sound caught her attention and sent cold fear racing through her. She listened but heard nothing more. The noise seemed to have come from a storage room on the right, probably nothing more than a mouse scurrying through, she told herself, moving slowly toward it.

Too late to back away, she found herself in the doorway, looking at the roustabout, the man she'd seen in the princess's tent. Slavko! In his hand was the necklace, and as he snatched something from his lap, she saw a picture. "You!" she cried.

Slavko leapt to his feet. "Who are you? What do you want with me?" Almost imperceptibly he inched toward her.

72

Trembling and without thinking, Jeanmarie blurted out, "You're the man I saw in the tent, the one with the princess's necklace."

Slavko moved so quickly Jeanmarie had no time to escape. "So," he said, grabbing her arm and holding it fast. "How did you find me? What are you doing down here? Who is with you? And why are you following me?" He pulled her into the room while he secured the necklace and picture inside his shirt with his free hand.

"Let me go," Jeanmarie cried, "or I'll scream." She struggled to free herself, kicking hard at Slavko's legs. In her heart she cried out to God for help.

"No one comes down here, and no one can hear you if you do scream. Be still, and I will let you go," Slavko said. "I am not going to harm you." As Jeanmarie continued to strike at him he shouted at her. "I can explain everything if you stop."

Little by little Jeanmarie became still, as if someone else, not Slavko, were calming her inside. Gradually, Slavko loosened his hold. She wanted to run but instead heard herself shouting, "Alright, explain why you stole the necklace and the picture!"

Slavko had released her arm but moved back to stand between her and the doorway. "Please, I never meant to hurt anyone. I was already planning to leave the circus the day you saw me in the tent. With the fire and all the panic everywhere, I too lost my sense. I knew it would be my chance to have something that belonged to the princess. When I saw the necklace, the one she liked to wear in the parade, I took it. It is glass, worth nothing, but to me priceless."

"And what about the picture?" Jeanmarie boldly demanded. She hadn't meant to blurt it out, but she couldn't help herself.

Slavko hung his head for a moment. "I took the picture earlier. It seemed to me that though the princess would not have me, I deserved something. I hoped to leave as soon as the circus finished here."

He was still blocking the door. If only he would leave. "Then why didn't you go the day of the fire? Why are you down here?" she cried, only half realizing that she was asking the questions instead of answering Slavko's.

A shadow of pain passed across his face. "I could not go so easily. When I learned that the princess had serious wounds from the cats and was here, I had to see her. Before going to visit her, I was on my way to quit the circus when I overheard voices inside the boss's wagon. They were talking about me." Slavko shifted uneasily. "Someone said they had seen me hanging around near the tents during the fire. Worse, they suggested that I might have set the fire. Everyone knew of my quarrel with Willie over the princess." A hard look came over his face. "How could they think I would deliberately set a fire while her act was going on in the ring? I would not do such a thing," he said. "I knew they would go to the police with their story, and so I left before anyone saw me."

Jeanmarie raised her eyebrows. So Willie the clown and Slavko the roustabout had fought over the princess. She didn't tell Slavko that Willie knew about the necklace and was looking for him. "But you stole the picture and the necklace," Jeanmarie accused.

Slavko ran his hand across his eyes. "I never meant to steal, only to have something of hers, a keepsake. Now it has all come to this. I am a thief wanted by the police, and they think I set that fire to the big top. It is a hopeless mess."

He looked so anguished that Jeanmarie almost forgot her fear. "But anyone might have set the fire," she said. "Don't you know that the fire chief thinks someone in the men's room of the side tent lit a cigarette in there, probably tossed it, and started the fire? The big top was covered with a mixture of melted wax and gasoline to waterproof it, so all it took was a spark to set the whole thing going."

"A cigarette in the men's room?" Slavko said, looking at her in amazement. "But none of the circus crew use that room, and I don't even smoke. But why should the police believe me?" he questioned.

"I don't know," Jeanmarie said. "But the newspapers say anyone could have done it accidentally, and the real blame is on the men responsible for putting flammable stuff on the tent in the first place. But you did steal, and what you did was wrong," she added. She could have bitten her tongue, but the words were already out.

"I know," Slavko agreed. "I was wrong. And once I am certain Princess will not suffer infection from the cats I will leave and never return. But now . . . ," he hesitated, then straightened stiffly. "You have not yet told me what you are doing down here and who was with you in the church."

Jeanmarie felt her stomach sink. She'd forgotten Pearl, who was waiting alone in the chapel. "I have to go back quickly," she said. "My blind friend is in the chapel by herself. By now she will be panicking, unless . . . ," she faltered.

"Unless what?" Slavko suddenly demanded.

"I might as well tell you that Wilfred, a boy from the orphanage where I live, broke his arm in the circus fire, and he knows about you. When I said I saw you down here the other day"—at her words Slavko's face darkened—"the three of us planned to come down and look for clues. We thought we ought to tell the princess. Wilfred went to find her. He should be back any time now." She hoped the fact that the princess was coming with Wilfred might make Slavko decide to leave and let her go back to Pearl.

"The princess's room is through the main tunnel on the next floor; which way did your friend go?"

Slavko's question surprised her. She'd expected a different reaction. Why did he want to know which way Wilfred had gone? "He took the left fork of the main corridor down here near the chapel," she said haltingly

"Is he a dark-haired boy with glasses?" Slavko asked.

"Yes, but how did you know?" she said.

Slavko's face paled. "Your friend won't be coming with Princess," he said. "He is lying at the foot of a collapsed stairway along an old abandoned tunnel way. I was on my way to get rope or something to use to reach him when I heard you and your friend in the church. I panicked and ran here for the necklace and picture, but I would have gone back for the boy if you hadn't come."

Jeanmarie's throat felt dry and her voice weak. "You should have told me. We have to help him, please." Wilfred already had a broken arm. What if he was badly hurt? A feeling of weakness came over her, making her legs tremble, and pain squeezed her side. "Let me go for help," she begged. Slavko looked down, and she couldn't see his eyes. Would he let her go? She'd have to get to Pearl too. "We have to find help, please," she begged.

Slavko pressed a hand to his head as if trying to decide what to do. "By the time help comes it may be too late. He is half-buried already, and more of the wall could fall at any time and smother him. We must help your friend now. There is no time to lose. I will get tools from the storage room near the church. Both you and your blind friend must help me. Come." It was not exactly true that more of the old wall would come down, though the edge around the hole was weak. But he could not afford to wait for others to come. There would surely be police involved who would question how he came to be down there. He would do whatever he could to reach the boy and free him; after that he would leave them on their own and make his escape. The girl had courage. She would find help. Swiftly he led the way back to the chapel.

Jeanmarie hurried as fast as she could after Slavko. "Please, God, don't let the rest of the wall fall on Wilfred." How would they ever get out of this whole mess? Why hadn't Slavko told her about Wilfred right away? They'd already wasted so much time. It hurt her side to hurry, but she pressed her hand against her bandages, gritted her teeth, and pushed on. She could see the chapel room ahead.

TEN

In the Dark

Pearl wrapped her arms close to her body. The dampness had grown uncomfortably cool. She listened hard for footsteps but heard nothing. Jeanmarie should have been right back. It was just like her to go chasing after that man. Why didn't she think to warn her? The man was dangerous, and what if he saw her? Jeanmarie could be in trouble. Maybe that's why she hadn't come back. Pearl pressed her hands against the pew in front of her. What should she do? Suddenly the darkness and silence felt full of danger. If she made her way to the door and then felt her way along the wall to the elevator she could go for help. But suppose the man saw her? She wouldn't know until it was too late. The thought of not seeing her pursuer sent a shiver down her spine. She wanted to curl into a ball and hide herself under the pew. "Help me, dear God. What should I do?" she said softly.

78

A sudden thought popped into her head. Miss Bigler, the assistant superintendent at the orphanage, had come to visit her in the hospital. Her words came back to Pearl now. "The Bible says that even the darkness is not dark to God. Why the night is as bright as the day, and the darkness just like light to him," she'd said. Pearl whispered, "God, I know you can see everything right now, but I can't see anything, and I'm afraid."

As if to answer her, something else Miss Bigler had said came to her. "Remember how God helped his children in the Bible?" she'd said. Pearl began thinking about the Bible story of Joseph, the boy who'd been thrown into a pit to die. And then his own brothers had sold him into slavery. While he was a slave Joseph had been arrested for a crime he didn't commit and thrown into prison. But God had made a way for Joseph to be freed and even made him a great ruler in Egypt. In her mind Pearl heard Miss Bigler's voice: "God doesn't desert us when we don't understand things that happen. Trust him." Pearl clung desperately to the words. Her bandaged eyes had no tears, but a dry sob escaped her throat.

She listened for a while, hoping to hear Jeanmarie coming. The thought that Wilfred and Jeanmarie would probably be here any minute comforted her. She had better stay put in the old chapel.

Turning her head toward the place where she thought the stained glass windows with the angels were that Jeanmarie had described, Pearl forced herself to think of angels watching over the old chapel. Whoever placed them in the windows must have meant that. "Think of all the good things," she told herself. She remembered the two large candlesticks in front of the angel windows near the altar. The old candles were still in them. Of course they weren't lit, but that didn't make any difference to her now.

If only she could see! Pearl whispered, "Dear God, please help me." She wouldn't let herself think bad things. Running her fingers over the back of the pew in front of her she felt the smoothness of the old wood. "It's sort of like seeing with my hands," she told herself. But what good would it do? Shivering, she wrapped her arms close to her chest and sat rigid, listening for any sound of footsteps, but there were none.

With her back pressed against the pew there was not much space for her knees between it and the back of the next pew. Long ago when the chapel was new someone must have sat here. "Think," she demanded. She began to imagine a girl with blonde hair and blue eyes sitting in the pew and patients and their families all around her. A slight sound made her freeze and listen, but there was nothing, only the silence. Either she had imagined it or whatever it was had gone. She forced herself to go on thinking about the girl in the past. There would be a minister, a tall man in a long, black robe. He would lead the singing. Pearl thought of the old songs she'd heard and remembered one called "Sweet Sounds of Praise and Thanks Arise."

Remembering the words, she whispered the first verse, pausing on the second verse to think of the words. "Bless all who slumber, all who wake," she sang softly. The sound of Jeanmarie's voice interrupted her.

"You're back!" Pearl cried.

"Oh, Pearl, you're alright," Jeanmarie said hugging her.

"Better use that wheelchair for your friend," a man's voice commanded.

"Who's with you?" Pearl asked, jerking her head toward the strange voice.

Jeanmarie clutched Pearl's hand as she said, "It's Slavko, but there's no time to explain. We've got to help Wilfred. A stairway collapsed in the old part of the building, and he's fallen into a deep hole."

"Wilfred? But what about the tunnel . . . and the princess?" Pearl asked in a confused voice.

"Wilfred must have mistaken an old abandoned tunnel for the new one," Jeanmarie said as she helped Pearl into the wheelchair. A strong hand gripped the handle. Grateful, Jeanmarie let Slavko wheel the heavy chair.

"I don't understand!" Pearl cried. "What's going on?"

"I found the boy, and your friend found me while I was going for something to use to reach him," Slavko said. He made it sound simple, and it wasn't. But at the moment Jeanmarie didn't care, not with Wilfred's life in danger. Slavko stopped the chair inside the storage room next to a pile of pieces of wood, bits of wire, old light sockets, and things Jeanmarie didn't recognize. Workmen had obviously discarded the items down here. As he searched through the pile for what he wanted, he explained. "I will do what I can for your friend Wilfred, but you two must help me. There is no time to lose. We may already be too late."

Jeanmarie felt her stomach sink. "Wouldn't it be better if I took Pearl and went for help," she said, "while you stay with Wilfred?"

Slavko continued to rummage through the junk on the floor. "I will need your help, and there is no time left to waste. Your friend is in serious trouble," he said, looking up. "We must get him out, and then you can go for help."

Pearl felt for Jeanmarie's hand and clutched it. "Is it true?"

Jeanmarie bit her lip. "We have to trust him," she whispered.

"But what if he's lying?" Pearl said, her voice low and trembling.

Slavko held up a thin coil of rope. "This rope will have to do," he said, hanging it on the wheelchair handle. "It's all I can find. Come. We must hurry."

Jeanmarie stared at Slavko. Why wouldn't he let her go for help? Was he telling the truth? Would he leave the two of them tied up somewhere down here? Slavko's eyes were unreadable, and even as she searched them she prayed, "What should we do, Lord?" Slavko took hold of the wheelchair to push it.

Jeanmarie's hands trembled, and her mind raced. She remembered a Bible verse she knew well: "When I am afraid, I will put my trust in you." She was afraid now. If she ran, Slavko would follow her, and even if he didn't catch her, what about Pearl? Worse, what about Wilfred? The thought of Wilfred made her eyes fill with tears. Slavko was looking at her, waiting. Her voice sounded small and thin as she said, "Yes, please, hurry."

ELEVEN

Cave-in

*I*nside the old tunnel they went single file, Jeanmarie following Slavko. The air in the tunnel held coolness, the smell of earth, and musty oldness. Her thoughts raced. What if they were making a terrible mistake? Should she go for help? This was her chance. She could turn around and run for the main corridor and the nearest elevator while Slavko was ahead of her. He might not even miss her until the end of the tunnel. But with each step she knew she couldn't leave Pearl.

"Here!" Slavko called.

They entered a large room, and in the dim light Jeanmarie saw the gaping hole ahead; it was true. "Wilfred!" she cried, running forward.

Instantly Slavko grabbed her by the arm. "No."

"Let me go!" Jeanmarie shouted, pulling with all her might. Fear that Slavko had betrayed them blotted out everything else.

"What are you doing?" Pearl cried. "Don't hurt her." In her anguish she stood, sending the chair flying backwards.

"I am trying to save her from falling in too," Slavko said, holding Jeanmarie firmly. "The edge is weakened. We must go carefully, slowly, and not too close. Do you understand?" Just as he spoke, a small bit of the lip around the hole broke away and fell in. Trembling, Jeanmarie stopped struggling. She stood quietly and nodded her head.

"Are you all right?" Pearl asked in an anxious voice.

"Yes, but he's right, the dirt is loose around the edge of the hole. You better stay back, Pearl."

Slavko walked to the wheelchair, brought it to Pearl, and helped her into it. "I must have forgotten to set the brake," he said, moving the brake handle into place. "There, it is fixed. You will be safe. Sit and pray that we all will be, and the boy especially."

Staying clear of several wide cracks near the hole, Jeanmarie inched her way on hands and knees toward the edge as far as she could go safely to peer down. "Wilfred!" she called, looking below at the barely visible boy half-buried under a pile of stones and dirt. "It's me, Jeanmarie." She couldn't tell if he was conscious or not. He was still wearing his glasses; they were dark against his white face, and she could see his arm in its white cast and sling. "Answer me," she demanded. Please, please, she begged silently, don't let him be dead.

"Cold," came a small, hoarse voice. Wilfred!

"We're coming!" Jeanmarie cried loudly. "Hold on. You're going to be alright; just hold on. We're here."

Slavko had come to the edge beside her. "Thank God, he is still alive," he said. "With the rope I can slide down, attach it to him, climb back up, and together we can pull him up. The end of the rope is tied with a good strong knot to a pipe on the wall by the doorway. It was the only thing I could find. Better move away now until I tell you it is safe." Gently Slavko lowered the rope into the hole.

Jeanmarie crawled backwards until she could stand. Quickly she went to Pearl and took her hand. "Wilfred knows we're here. He said he's cold. I'm sure it's shock. Slavko is climbing down into the hole now with the rope." The next minute came with a loud crash. Something flew past, narrowly missing them—the pipe with the rope! Like a spear it flew directly into the hole. A terrible cry from the pit froze Jeanmarie with fear. "The wall!" she cried.

When the dust settled, it was not the wall but a section of the ledge where Slavko had gone over that had fallen in, enlarging the hole and yanking the old pipe and rope with it.

"What happened?" Pearl cried, clutching Jeanmarie's arm.

"A cave-in," Jeanmarie said. "The hole is wider than ever, and the rope fell into it too. Stay here," she commanded, "until I see what's happened."

"Be careful," Pearl begged.

"I won't go near the edge, only far enough to see inside. If I *can* see anything in all this dust." She covered her mouth with her hand, leaving just enough room to call, "Slavko, are you alright?"

For a few seconds she heard nothing as she crawled nearer to the edge. It was hopeless. The dirt floor in front of her was cracked and looked dangerous. She didn't dare go closer. "Slavko, Wilfred?" she called.

"Alive, so far," came back. The voice was Slavko's. "I think my leg is broken," he said. "The boy is still conscious. You will have to get help. Go back the way we came through the short tunnel to the corridor and take the first elevator you find. Call for help. Tell them there has been a cave-in. They will know what to do." He groaned.

"Wilfred, what about Wilfred?" Jeanmarie insisted. "Why isn't he saying anything?"

"He's alive," Slavko called back. "I am digging him out with my bare hands. We will need lots of blankets and a stretcher. Now go!"

"Right!" Jeanmarie shouted. Once safely back by Pearl she hesitated. If Pearl walked they could both go for help. Only by herself she would make better time.

It was as if her best friend, blind or not, knew what Jeanmarie was thinking. "You go. I'll stay here with Slavko and Wilfred. It's the least I can do," Pearl said.

When Jeanmarie's footsteps no longer came to her, Pearl listened to the sound of Slavko's digging, a faint plunking of stones. He must be throwing them off Wilfred, she thought. More than once she heard the pain in Slavko's voice when he cried out as he worked in spite of his injured leg. Pearl gripped the arms of the wheelchair tightly, feeling the strain. "Dear God, help them," she whispered. And then she began to sing, softly at first, but louder and stronger as the words came to her, "O God, our help in ages past. . . ." To her amazement she suddenly found another voice faint and faltering but singing the very words with her—Slavko singing in the pit.

When she had sung all the verses she knew, Pearl called out, "Slavko, how is it going?"

"Slowly," he replied. "The boy is almost free. He is so cold. I have covered him with my shirt but he needs more and soon."

Pearl felt her way out of her hospital robe and let her fingers find the sleeves. She pressed the robe into a lump and tied the sleeves around it. "Slavko," she cried, "I'm throwing my robe down to you for Wilfred."

"Wait," Slavko called back, fear in his voice. "You must not come too close to the edge. I cannot help you if you fall."

Pearl stood up with one hand holding the wheelchair. "What if I push the chair in front of me slowly," she said, "and when you see it, say stop. I can throw the robe from there."

"The chair will move straight ahead if you do not turn it. A straight line will keep you away from the weakened part of the ledge. Listen now, you must count your steps one at a time and walk slowly until I tell you to stop," Slavko commanded.

Pearl felt her way to the back of the chair, found the brake, and released it. "Okay then, here I come." Pushing the chair with each step and counting as she went, she shuffled step-by-step slowly until she reached nineteen. Slavko's voice rang out, halting her. Pearl squeezed the robe tightly and drew back her arm as she did when pitching ball back at the orphanage ball field. "Say something," she said. At the sound of Slavko's voice she threw the robe. A cry of triumph came back.

"Now I have something to send up to you. If I'm lucky, I will land the princess's necklace right in the seat of your wheelchair."

A sudden clunk made Pearl lean over to feel the chair seat. Hard round stones and chain pressed against her fingers as she felt them. "I have it," she called.

"Good," Slavko said. "I'm afraid the picture would not do as well. The frame is already damaged, but at least the princess shall have her necklace back." His voice seemed to catch and then became firm again. "Listen to me carefully," he said. "How many steps did you count?"

"Nineteen," Pearl answered.

"Right. Then you must go backwards exactly nineteen steps with the chair. Set the brake before you sit down again. You might sing something. It helps."

On the nineteenth step Pearl stopped the chair she had pulled backwards with her, set the brake, and feeling her way, sat down in it. The necklace she slid around her neck. What should she sing? A song that was a favorite with the little girls back in the orphanage came to her lips, "Jesus loves me, this I know, for the Bible tells me so," she began.

TWELVE

Nellie Finds a Way

Jeanmarie pressed both hands against her side as she hurried. In her mind she saw poor Wilfred lying pale and still at the bottom of the hole. Now Slavko too was trapped down there. "Have to keep going no matter what," she whispered. Though she couldn't run she pushed herself to an awkward kind of fast walk, but already she felt like a runner out of breath. The shortcut tunnel ended abruptly, only now which way to the elevator?

From where she stood she could see no sign of one. Slavko had said "take the first elevator you find." Okay, but do I go left or right? She tried to remember which way went back toward the old chapel. "Think," she told herself. Nothing! "Maybe it was to the right." Somewhere down that corridor there had to be an elevator. She hurried to the right.

The hall turned sharply, and a few feet ahead she saw the elevator. It was larger than any she'd seen before, probably the one used for hauling big equipment; all she needed was for it to work. The door closed, but before she could press one of the buttons the elevator started. Someone must have pressed a button upstairs. Jeanmarie felt her heart racing. The only thing she had to do now was tell whoever it was to get help.

The door opened, and Jeanmarie stared in disbelief. Nellie stood in front of the elevator, grinning. Jeanmarie's mind seemed to freeze as Nellie gripped her arm and pulled her into the hallway. "You shouldn't be riding the freight elevator, you know," she said loudly. "I'll show you where the other one is," she insisted, keeping her strong hold on Jeanmarie's arm.

"I can't come now," Jeanmarie said, frantically looking for someone to help her. The hall was empty, but behind Nellie a door with a metal grating across its glass window opened and a man stepped out. He was obviously one of the staff because he was wearing a white uniform. Jeanmarie breathed a sigh of relief.

"Now, Nellie," he said, coming toward them, "I may be new here, but I've heard all about you, and you better come back inside where you're supposed to be. Don't know how you managed to get out here." He shook his head. "I see you've brought a friend with you this time." He reached one hand to grasp Nellie's arm and another to grip Jeanmarie's. "Why don't you just be good and stay put? We don't have time to play this game today," he said.

"Please," Jeanmarie cried. "There's no time. I got on the elevator to go for help, and Nellie pushed the button before I could. This isn't my floor. I need to find help." Her words tumbled out rapidly. "There's been a cave-in down in the basement, and a boy and a man are trapped down there. There's a blind girl with them too in a wheelchair. Please, you have to help, and get others too. We need blankets and a stretcher," she added breathlessly. For a second her words sounded wild to her ears.

The man did not loosen his grip on her arm. "You calm down now. You leave it all in my hands. First we'll have to go inside." He opened the locked door with the metal grille and shooed Jeanmarie inside along with Nellie. The room looked like a large lounge to Jeanmarie. Patients were everywhere. Some just sat, some worked puzzles, others stood or walked. She knew right away that this was a ward for the mentally ill patients like Nellie.

"Now, Nellie, you just take your friend and have a seat. I have work to do."

He started to walk away, leaving Jeanmarie with Nellie.

Jeanmarie felt herself grow weak in the legs. The man didn't believe her. "But I don't belong here. You have to believe me! There's been a terrible accident, and people are hurt. You need to know how to find the others, and I'm the only one who can show the way. Wait, please!" Jeanmarie cried. She hurried after the man only to see him disappear into what looked like an office with a large glass window covered by a metal grille. The sound of the door lock clicked behind him.

"He didn't listen to me," Jeanmarie wailed.

Nellie had come to stand beside her. "Oh, he heard you, he just didn't believe you. He thinks you're another one of the patients," she said. "He's new around here. Short of help this place is most times. War on, you know. No use shouting at him. He'll just ignore you like he does the rest of us."

"He better listen to me," Jeanmarie said. With all her might she pounded on the office door. It was solid, and the man inside sitting at his desk paid no attention. Worse, an old man dressed in striped pajamas and a robe came to stand beside her and began to hit the door rhythmically as if it were a kind of drum. Jeanmarie backed away. She had to find someone who would listen to her. She had to get out of here.

As far as she could see there were no other staff attendants in the lounge, and patients moved freely about the room. At the far end she spotted a corridor and headed for it. Like a shadow Nellie followed right behind her. The long hall led to patients' sleeping quarters.

"Do you want to see my room?" Nellie asked.

Jeanmarie turned to face her. "Please leave me alone," she said. "What I want is to find a nurse or anyone who believes me." The strain had begun to tell on her and her eyes filled with tears.

"Won't find anyone. Two's gone to a meeting, won't be back for an hour. Nurse Potz, she had to take one of the patients to get his tooth pulled. Won't be back soon." Nellie reached into her dress pocket and pulled out a bit of cloth. "Here," she said, handing it to Jeanmarie.

The last thing she wanted was to share Nellie's handkerchief. She swiped at the spill of tears on her face with the back of her hand. "Thanks, I'm okay." She took a deep breath and let it out slowly. "I know you don't believe me, but there really was an accident, and if I don't get help Wilfred could die."

Nellie nodded. "Sure, I believe you. Didn't I see you down there last week? Or was it this week? I been down there lots of times. Seen the old tunnel and all them old rooms. Used to be they'd have kept us all down there but not anymore. Keep the really bad ones locked in a ward down the other end of this floor. Not so many of us in here and they give us our own room. Got my own room. You want to see it?"

Jeanmarie's thoughts whirled. "Nellie, you've been in the basement before, so you must know a way to get down there. Do you think I can get out of here and go back there? The way you did, I mean?" If only Nellie did know some escape route Jeanmarie could use she'd go back to her own floor and get help there.

Nellie looked at her with narrowed eyes. "Can't tell," she said.

"Why can't you tell me?" Jeanmarie asked. Her side had begun to ache, and she wanted to sit down.

Nellie shook her head. "Can't tell."

"But it's really important; please," Jeanmarie urged her. "Two people are badly hurt and need help quickly."

"Can't tell," Nellie said stubbornly, locking her arms across her chest.

"Never mind," Jeanmarie said. "I'll think of something. Right now I need to sit down somewhere." She didn't want to upset the woman, and she needed to think.

"You want to see my room?" Nellie asked again.

Jeanmarie ignored the question. "Are you sure there's no one else around I can ask for help? What if I break a window or something to get the man in the office to come out and listen to me?" She felt ready to do anything including beat on his door again; only why was she asking this woman questions when she obviously was a patient in the ward?

"Special glass, won't break, and he might put you in isolation till the others come back. Won't help you none," Nellie said. She took Jeanmarie's hand and began pulling her down the hall to the last room on the right. She sounded so rational that reluctantly Jeanmarie let herself be led.

The small room contained a bed, a nightstand, and a window with the usual grille cover. Nellie pointed to the bed. "Sit," she said.

Jeanmarie sat on the edge of the narrow cot. "Thanks," she said. She really felt grateful to sit down. "Is this your room?"

Nellie nodded. "Don't think they can't hear you in here," she said in a hushed voice. "Better keep your voice down just in case." Nellie took off her old sweater and draped it over the foot of the bed.

"How long have you been here?" Jeanmarie asked, keeping her voice low.

"Long," Nellie said. "Can't remember being outside anymore. Course I could go out if I wanted to, but there's a war on, you know. Safer in here. Used to it now anyway."

Jeanmarie looked around at the room; it was shabby with its bare walls and cracked ceiling. Nellie watched her closely. "I'm glad you have a window," Jeanmarie said, not knowing what Nellie expected. At least the barred window was large enough to let in the bright summer light, and she felt glad of it at the moment.

"Will you be my friend?" Nellie asked abruptly. "Ain't got any friends 'cept for George and Mary, and most times they just sit and stare at the walls. Wish I had a cross like that one you're wearing," she added.

Jeanmarie looked down at the cross. She had forgotten she was wearing it. Slowly she slipped it from her neck and handed it to Nellie. "Here; why don't you keep it," she said. Under all her desperate fears for Wilfred and the others, a feeling of sadness for Nellie washed over her like a small wave.

Lifting the cross on its leather chain over her head Nellie settled it around her neck. "That means we're friends. And friends don't tell on each other, they share. Agreed?" Nellie asked.

Jeanmarie leaned forward eagerly; was Nellie about to share her secret way to escape? "Agreed."

With her finger to her lips, Nellie pointed to the doorway and then whispered, "We won't ever tell them." She went to the doorway, looking first one way then the other. "It's clear; come on."

Jeanmarie stood and tiptoed to the door. What was Nellie doing? Turning right toward the far end of the corridor Nellie moved quickly. At the end she waited for Jeanmarie to catch up with her. "Follow me," Nellie said. Jeanmarie nodded. There was no one in the hall when Nellie made a lightning dash to the large door directly across from them, opened it, and flung herself inside.

"This is it," Jeanmarie thought, hurrying after Nellie. "Her escape route." Nellie had closed the door almost before Jeanmarie pushed her way in. "But this is a closet," she said. Brooms and pails and cleaning things leaned against the walls or hung from nails.

"No, no," Nellie whispered. "Feel this pipe on the wall? The floor around it is loose." She felt for Jeanmarie's hand and brought it to a large metal pipe.

As Jeanmarie knelt and let her hand slide down the metal to where it met the floor, she could feel air coming through near the floor. "Now what do we do?" she whispered.

Nellie's face was close to hers, and Jeanmarie could feel her warm breath.

"Keep low so you don't bang into anything and crawl backwards so I can move this piece of floor. It's all cut here in a nice big square around the pipe. That's the way the workmen did it," she explained. "Must have been a long time ago. Guess they did it so they could get to the pipe when they needed to. Just pull this up, and it gives lots of room. Put it back down just like a big plug when you finish. Fits right onto a little ledge all around. Nobody uses it anymore, and the only way to know it comes up is by that little space near the pipe. One day I just stuck my hand down there and that's when I discovered how it comes up nice and easy like a manhole cover."

So it was Nellie's escape route! "But where does it lead?" Jeanmarie whispered.

"Goes right on down into the closet on the next floor. Course you got to hold onto the pipe and slide careful. I moved a ladder underneath so it's easy to get down. You don't want to go falling and making noise. It's only good in the afternoon or night when all the cleaning's through for the day." Nellie stopped talking for a minute and then whispered, "I'll go on down first. Then you follow me. You got to be careful not to touch the plug 'cause I got to put it back in place."

Jeanmarie heard Nellie grunt and push and then suddenly she was gone. Holding her bandaged side, she felt for the open edge and the pipe. "I don't know if I can do this; I'm afraid the stitches in my side will burst. I just had my appendix out," she said in a low voice.

Nellie was still for a moment. "Then sit on the edge and just put your feet through. Hold the pipe with both hands and reach your feet down as far as you can. Soon as I feel your feet you can rest 'em on my shoulder. Then move your hands down the pipe as far as you can, and I'll help you stand on this stepladder."

"Okay," Jeanmarie said. Her legs felt like rubber and her hands trembled, but she grasped the thick pipe firmly and managed to put her feet into the hole. She could feel Nellie's hands grasp her ankles, and then she was leaning her weight on Nellie's shoulder. She slid her hands down the pipe. "Ready," she said.

Nellie's strong hands held her legs fast as she guided first one foot and then the other onto the top of the ladder. "That's it," Nellie said. "Now you climb down here so I can climb back up and close the hole. We don't want anybody finding that hole."

They exchanged places, and Jeanmarie sat on the closet floor holding her aching side. They were on the next floor. Surely someone would believe her and get help. But what about Nellie? The nurses all knew her. If Nellie was with her how would she explain? "This is a fine mess," she said aloud. "Here we are on another floor, but the nurses know you, Nellie. They'll send you back and think I made up the whole story."

"You promised not to tell," Nellie said in a loud whisper.

"I won't tell about this place; I promised. But how am I going to explain so that they will believe me about the cave-in?" Jeanmarie reached for Nellie's hand. "Nellie, I have to go out there alone and find help before the whole wall down there falls in on top of Wilfred and Slavko." The thought made her stomach knot. "Pearl is with them, but she's blind and she can't help them. Could you wait in here a while so no one sees us together, just long enough for me to get someone who can do something?"

"We're friends, aren't we? Friends stick by each other. It's what friends do. You go on and find a nurse or one of the doctors. I'll go on back up. Wasn't planning on coming down today anyway. Might be ice cream for dessert tonight. You go on." Nellie loosened her hand from Jeanmarie's. "Come on, I'll check the hallway for you. Know every inch of this here closet. Crawled my way around it plenty." A thin shaft of light entered as Nellie let the door crack open the tiniest bit. After a moment, she seemed satisfied and, opening it wider, motioned for Jeanmarie to go.

"You're a real friend, Nellie. Thanks," Jeanmarie whispered. In a second she was out of the closet. Behind her the door closed firmly. There were noises down the hall and the welcome sound of clattering trays. Holding her side she hurried toward the sounds.

THIRTEEN

The Imaginary Cane

*H*old on, settle down," the nurse on duty at the desk said firmly. "We've been looking all over for you. In fact you have two visitors who were just about to give up on your coming back in time."

"Visitors?" Jeanmarie looked at her, puzzled. "But you have to listen to me; there's no time," she pleaded.

"No time? Who needs time?" a booming voice said behind Jeanmarie. She turned to see Weary Willie the clown coming toward them with the princess on his arm.

Jeanmarie forgot her aching side as she cried out, "We have to help Wilfred and Slavko too. In the basement, the wall caved in and they're trapped." She was sobbing and trying to explain all at the same time. "You have to believe me; it's true."

On his knees with his arm around Jeanmarie's shoulder Willie listened then asked, "Do you think you can show me where they are?"

Jeanmarie nodded. "We were down by the old chapel. It's not far from there."

"That part of the building is ancient. I'll call security for help," the nurse said, running back to the desk. "That child shouldn't be walking around anywhere!" she called back.

"Please, I have to go. I can take you to them," Jeanmarie pleaded.

The princess pointed to a wheelchair near the desk. "We can push her in that," she said.

As Willie helped Jeanmarie into the chair, two security guards came running. "Over here!" Willie called. "There's been a cave-in near one of the old abandoned tunnels in the basement. Two people are trapped in there, one of them a boy, and from the sound of it he may be hurt bad. We'll need rope and ladders, lights, and a doctor," he added.

"You'll need an emergency crew down there with stretchers and blankets too," the nurse added. "I'll ring them now to meet you in the basement."

"Can you show us the way?" one of the guards asked. "It will save time if we don't have to look up the building plans to locate that tunnel."

"The girl knows where they are," Willie said.

Jeanmarie swallowed hard. "We have to take the freight elevator down," she said. At least she knew that was right. Would she remember the way once they were down there?

"They've been down there an awful long time," Jeanmarie said, looking up at the princess.

As they hurried to the elevator, the princess held Jeanmarie's hand. "You said Slavko is hurt also?" she said. "I do not understand how all of you came to be in the basement." As Jeanmarie explained, the princess covered her mouth and shook her head. "Poor children, poor unhappy Slavko. He would never harm anyone. If he could have saved the boy he would have. Oh, Willie, I feel like this is all my fault."

In the dark Pearl sat praying. She'd sung and sung, but at last Slavko's voice became still and then her own. Where was Jeanmarie with the help she had gone for? How long it seemed since she'd left.

"Slavko, are you there?" Pearl called. "Slavko?" She listened as fear gripped her. "Please don't let me be alone down here, please God," she prayed.

A tired voice came back to her. "Yes, I am here. But where is your friend? She should have been back long ago," he said. "The boy is not doing well. We must get help."

"What can we do?" Pearl cried. "Jeanmarie will come. I know she would never leave us here without help. Oh, do you think she's lost?" The idea had come to her strongly in the last little while.

"She cannot be lost," Slavko said harshly. "Time is running out. Listen to me, Pearl. You must go for help. I will tell you exactly what to do."

"But you know I can't see. I can't help," she cried.

"Your friend is in grave danger. You can do this. Remember how you counted the steps and threw your robe to us? It will be like that," Slavko said.

"I'll try," Pearl said.

"Good; now listen carefully. When I wheeled you here in the chair you did not know that we passed through a short tunnel from the main corridor. The tunnel opens into this room. The opening is right behind your chair. Picture it in your mind."

"Yes, I see it," Pearl called.

Slavko's voice was firm and clear like a schoolteacher's. "What I want you to do is stand behind your chair with your back against it. Please do this now."

Carefully Pearl felt her way around the chair. "I'm doing it," she said. "But what do I do now?"

"Now," Slavko said, "with your right hand feel the wall next to you. Let your left hand pretend it is holding a walking cane."

"Yes!" Pearl shouted. "I have it." Her left hand closed around an imaginary cane.

"That is how you will walk—right hand always on the wall, left holding your cane. When you no longer feel the wall on your right you will be at the entrance to the main corridor. Picture yourself walking through the tunnel and coming to its end." He paused.

When Pearl was ready she called, "Got it."

"Remember that your left hand is holding your cane," Slavko said. "Now you are at the end of the tunnel and you will raise your cane and hold it out straight in front of you, then walk straight ahead with it slowly till your cane hand feels the wall ahead of you. That will be the corridor wall straight across from the tunnel exit. Picture it."

After a moment Pearl said, "Ready."

"Then you will place your right hand on the corridor wall, bring your cane hand down, and begin walking again, right hand, never, I repeat, never leaving the wall. Left hand holding that cane as you walk one step at a time. You will come to an elevator door that your right hand will feel. The door will be set in a little ways, and you will find the elevator button about the height of your shoulder. Once you are on the elevator you may press any of the buttons. Wherever it stops you will find someone to help us. Now recite for me this plan as you picture it in your mind."

Starting at the beginning and picturing herself each step of the way, Pearl repeated Slavko's instructions.

"Good, very good. Now go, and God be with you," Slavko said.

"I'm leaving now," Pearl called out as she took the first timid step away from the back of her chair.

She found herself counting her steps, forty-nine, fifty. If only I had a real cane, she thought. Any minute she expected to stumble on a stone or worse. She stood still and listened, her right hand against the damp wall. The silence made her nervous. The air in the abandoned tunnel smelled earthy, and she wondered why it had never been finished. Did anyone else ever come down here? She walked on, trying to concentrate and listen at the same time. Her left hand cramped. She'd been holding it in a tight fist around the imaginary cane. The sudden feeling of something hairy and slightly sticky under her right hand changed everything.

She pulled her hand away from the wall quickly and rubbed it against her hospital gown. "Get away; get away!" she cried, slapping her hand against herself and shaking the gown hard. For good measure she felt her arm and then the front of her gown. She felt nothing. Had it been a spider or just a cobweb? How could she go on touching the wall? Tears of frustration ran down her face. She couldn't do this. "God, I can't do it, I can't do it," she prayed. "Help me, please, God." In the silence a thought came to her. Instead of her hand, maybe she could feel her way with her slippered foot by walking close enough to the bottom of the wall with her right foot next to it.

It took her a while to inch her way back to the wall. Had she turned around? She hoped not. She tried not to think of what else might be on the tunnel wall, but at least her slipper would help. Intent on not letting the wall touch any part of her except her foot, she was totally unprepared for the sudden wrenching as her foot went deep into some kind of hole. She fell, her hands flinging out too late to save her.

In a panic to free her foot she kicked free and rolled over well away from the wall. For several minutes she sat on the tunnel floor curled up in a tight ball with her hand on her knees and wept. When she finally grew still, something Princess had said came to her. "Thank God for the gifts you have." Practice and determination, Princess had said. "Sorry, God," she whispered. "I'm sitting here like a big baby, with two perfectly good feet to get me where I have to go." She stood, waited until she felt ready, and then felt once more for the wall with her right hand.

"I hope I'm facing the right way," she whispered. If not she'd end up back with the wheelchair and have to start again. "I need help," she said. "And, please," she added, "keep Wilfred and Slavko safe." This time she knew what to do. Not too hard, just enough to send notice that she was coming, she tapped the wall with her hand as she moved along it. "Hear me, spiders; get out of the way, 'cause I'm coming through!" she said loudly.

Something felt different. She could feel the air on her face and knew it felt warmer. The smell was different, not so earthy here. Carefully she continued moving, and suddenly she felt it—the end of the wall. "Now, cane up," she said, bringing her left hand straight out in front of her. "March." She went slowly, counting the steps out loud. "Got it!" she cried as her hand contacted with solid stone in front of her. She felt how the stones fit together and knew it was the wall. With her right hand on the stones and the imaginary cane in her left hand, she began walking. In her mind she pictured the way the wall would turn slightly to meet the elevator door.

Wilfred moaned, opened his eyes, and shut them again. Someone was holding him. Wilfred tried to speak, but the effort sent pain stabbing through him. He stopped.

Slavko sat with Wilfred's head against his chest and his arms about the boy, trying to give him some warmth from his body. He didn't dare move for fear of hurting him. Each movement had made the boy cry out, and from the swelling and odd angle of the boy's hand, the wrist was either broken or badly strained. Worse, he feared broken ribs and damage to the boy's shoulder either from his fall or the heavy stones and dirt that had toppled onto him.

Bending his head close to the boy's white face, Slavko felt the skin. Cold. Too cold. He spoke softly. "Can you hear me? Pearl has gone for help and your friend Jeanmarie too. They are coming soon. You are safe now. I am holding you tight. Think of how you will soon be back with your friends. You must be strong. Be strong for your friends." Slavko thought he saw the boy's eyes open, but they shut quickly. "I will sing a song for you," he said. "It is a song from my country about a brave hero." He began to sing. Wilfred heard the singing, and he listened.

Slavko was still singing when the others arrived.

FOURTEEN

Lost and Found

The elevator lurched along slowly, while Jeanmarie's thoughts raced ahead. What if they were too late? If only Nellie hadn't stopped her on the freight elevator Wilfred and Slavko might be rescued by now. Or better still if she'd turned left instead of right in the main corridor and taken the regular elevator, she'd never have run into Nellie at all. She shook her head. Who could have imagined it? And if Nellie hadn't shared her secret escape route she might not even be down here yet! A picture of herself climbing through the closet floor with Nellie holding her steady as if it were all a game flashed through her mind. It was as if some part of Nellie had never grown up. Jeanmarie pressed her lips together and tried to concentrate. She was supposed to know where they were going, but which way should they go from this elevator? Aloud she said, "When we leave the elevator we turn right, no, left, I mean."

The princess looked at her closely. "Take your time," she whispered. "Try to picture yourself coming from the tunnel." Jeanmarie nodded and closed her eyes and tried, but the corridor in her mind kept changing. "Left, I think," she said again, not sure. She tried to think as the elevator screeched to a halt. When the door opened, Jeanmarie gasped. Not two feet away stood Pearl, her right hand against the wall, her left held out in front of her.

"Jeanmarie, is that you?" Pearl cried.

"We're here," Jeanmarie shouted. "Willie, the princess, all of us."

The princess was already holding Pearl's hand and comforting her. "Help is on the way," she assured her. "Oh," she exclaimed suddenly. "My necklace. But where did you find it?" She touched a ruby stone hanging down the front of Pearl's gown.

Pearl felt the necklace, lifted it over her head, and held it out. "It's yours. Slavko gave it to me to keep for you. He's in the hole with Wilfred. I think his leg is broken."

"What's going on here?" one of the security guards with Jeanmarie demanded, frowning.

Pearl explained quickly. "And so when no one came, Slavko sent me to find help. We thought you were lost. Slavko told me what to do, and I pictured it all. I did fall one time, but I made it! I was almost to the elevator when I heard your voices," she finished.

Jeanmarie had left her chair and hurried to take Pearl's hand. "Don't worry, there's help now and more on the way," she said. She gripped Pearl's hand tightly. "I didn't think anyone would believe me; it was so awful," she choked on her words for a second. "But everything's going to be alright now, only we have to hurry. There's a wheelchair for you if you want to ride," she offered.

"No, I can walk," Pearl insisted.

Willie reached out a large hand and firmly planted Jeanmarie in the wheelchair. "Sit," he commanded. "I propel, you lead." With Jeanmarie in the chair he raced ahead, the security guards running behind him. The princess, holding Pearl's hand, hurried after them.

They could hear Slavko singing, something about a brave boy, as they entered the big room. "We're here," Jeanmarie cried.

Slavko stopped singing. "Thank God," he said. "The wall seems to be stable, but the ledge is weak. You need rope and ladders and a stretcher for the boy," he added.

One of the security guards stayed while the other ran back through the tunnel to wait for the rescue team. Willie was already lying flat near the edge of the hole, his long legs grasped in the princess's strong hands as she knelt behind him. "Slavko, you okay?" Willie called down.

"Okay, with one broken leg," Slavko said. "I tried sliding down here on an old piece of rope tied to a pipe on the wall up there. The pipe gave way and struck my leg with a vengeance."

"Justice, my friend. But when I trounce you for the stolen necklace and picture, I'll tie one hand behind my back," Willie said. "How's the boy?"

"Not good," Slavko said. "His skin is cold, and I think he's got broken ribs, maybe a break in the wrist and shoulder, and I don't know what else. I could use blankets down here. I've been trying to keep him warm."

"Hold on, man," Willie said. "There's hope for you yet. Maybe I won't need to trounce you after all if you keep acting like a hero. Here come the troops. It won't be long before we have you both out of there."

A doctor, two nurses, and a maintenance man had come back with the guard, bringing stretchers, blankets, flashlights, and a ladder. As Jeanmarie and Pearl stood together, it seemed to take forever. After a small shower of dirt and stones from the ledge, one of the maintenance men managed to place a ladder and lean it against the wall that seemed firmest. A nurse had already thrown down blankets to Slavko. The doctor was the first to climb down after the maintenance man.

Jeanmarie could feel her heart beating. She took a deep breath when the doctor called for a stretcher and plenty of rope. When the guards pulled the stretcher out of the hole she knew the small frame lashed to it was Wilfred's. "Wilfred!" she cried, but there was no answer.

The doctor was already giving orders as he climbed out of the hole. "This boy needs immediate attention. We have to get him straight to emergency. Go, men, go," he ordered the two guards carrying the stretcher. One of the nurses went with them. "The man down there has a broken leg. He'll survive." He turned to the other nurse standing near the maintenance man. "Stay here, please. I'll send the guards back to help." Helpless to do anything for Wilfred, Jeanmarie felt like sobbing. "Please, God, don't let him die," she begged silently.

Willie spoke. "Doctor, this fellow and I will get him out. Just save the boy."

The doctor nodded. "Bring that one to the emergency as soon as you can. Watch yourself down there." He hurried into the tunnel.

The maintenance man held the ladder for Willie then followed him down. Jeanmarie heard a loud groan. Beside her the princess smothered a cry.

"We'll need the other stretcher!" Willie called up. "Princess, do you think you can lift the stretcher and pass it down the

109

ladder to me? You know, of course, if you're not careful you could bury us all down here or even slide down yourself."

"If I do," the princess said, "you had better catch me if you know what's good for you." Her face was pale as she picked up the stretcher with the help of the nurse. "Pearl, you and Jeanmarie must not go near the ledge no matter what happens; promise me." Jeanmarie nodded.

"I don't plan on getting this uniform dirty," the nurse said with a half-grin. "You two keep praying."

Moving slowly, searching the floor in front of her, the princess neared the edge where the top of the ladder rose just above the hole. "If we go single file with the stretcher between us, I think there will be less strain near the edge." Behind her the nurse agreed. "Now, lift with me, and I will let my end down over the ladder," the princess said. "Slowly, slowly, now let go," she ordered.

"Got it!" Willie cried. After several groans and grunts, the stretcher was lifted once more over the ladder and sent sliding away from the edge by a strong push from Willie.

Quickly with the princess's help the nurse dragged the stretcher well away from the hole.

Jeanmarie heard Slavko's voice as he saw the princess. "I'm sorry about the necklace, the picture, everything," he said.

"I know, Slavko. But I have my necklace back, and the picture I will give to you. Now get well so you can go home," she said.

Jeanmarie was close enough to see Slavko's tears. She could feel wetness on her own face. Whatever Slavko had done, she could only feel sorry for him.

Pearl groped with her hand to find the stretcher. "I made it, Slavko," she said. "You are one good teacher. I'll never forget you. Please get well."

"You will do okay," he said.

Jeanmarie looked at the princess, who smiled first at her then at Slavko. "And you too, Slavko," she said. "Back home you were the gifted one, the best guide in our village. Think about your gift from God, and get well soon."

"Time to go," the nurse ordered. "This man's leg needs attention."

Jeanmarie sighed. She felt a chill as she remembered Wilfred's pale face, his still form on the stretcher. "Please, please, God, help him." They were on their way to the emergency room with Slavko on the stretcher carried between Willie and the maintenance man. The princess was pushing her wheelchair, and Pearl walked at her side, holding one handle. Jeanmarie felt desperately tired, and her bandaged side throbbed. If only she knew what was happening to Wilfred. There was only one, brilliant, kindhearted, patient Wilfred in the orphanage, and they couldn't lose him. "Please, don't let him die," she prayed. In the emergency room attendants quickly whisked Slavko away, leaving Jeanmarie and Pearl to wait in a small waiting room. Willie and the princess talked briefly to the receptionist.

"Is Wilfred going to be alright?" Jeanmarie asked as Willie and the princess returned.

"His system has suffered shock, and he may have a punctured lung besides all his fractures. All we know is that his condition is serious. I'm afraid we'll have to wait until morning for more information," the princess said.

"As for you two, the nurse has allowed you the distinct honor of a noble escort back to your rooms, and may I present your most humble servant." Willie bowed low. "Weary Willie at your service." Jeanmarie laughed and groaned at the same time, holding her aching side.

Pearl, who had seen nothing but heard it all, held out her hand. "Charmed, I'm sure," she said.

Willie shook Pearl's hand. "Thank you, Mademoiselle," he said. "Say, does anybody know what time it is?" He fished inside his coat pocket and pulled out the most enormous timepiece Jeanmarie had ever seen. "Oh, there it is. I never can find this little thing." He took Pearl's hand and closed her fingers around part of the clock. "Mademoiselle, will you hold my little watch a moment?"

Pearl felt around the edges of the clock. "Oh," she said and laughed.

"Ah, past supper time by a long shot. I knew it," Willie said. "Thank you, Mademoiselle." He took the clock from Pearl and placed it back in his pocket. "So that's what my stomach's telling me, 'time to eat, time to eat.' Why don't I hunt up a little snack for all of us before I take you two back upstairs?"

Jeanmarie had forgotten all about food until now, and suddenly she felt famished. Somehow Willie found crackers, soda pop, pretzels, and even a bar of chocolate. They sat and ate in the emergency waiting room while Willie did his best to cheer everyone. "Time to go," he said as he stood. "The receptionist is giving me the evil eye."

"I'll wait here," the princess said. "At least until they've finished with Slavko. The police want to question him, and I'd like to be here."

When they reached the ward, Willie lightly kissed Jeanmarie's forehead. "If this clown had a sister, I should like one just like you," he said. "You have a grand gift for adventure, Jeanmarie. I think one day I'll be coming down Main Street and see a big sign: 'The Jeanmarie Detective Service, clowns free of course; everyone else pays.'"

"I'll remember," Jeanmarie said. She watched him lead Pearl down the hall. Her whole body ached with tiredness. The night shift nurse had fussed and scolded for a bit, but even she knew about Slavko and Wilfred and wanted to hear all the details. When the lights were finally out and quiet settled over the ward, Jeanmarie closed her eyes. She was weary beyond words, but sleep wouldn't come.

In the bed next to hers where the Spanish girl had been, a large red-haired woman snored in her sleep. Jeanmarie reached for the cross around her neck and remembered she had given it to Nellie. *"Vaya con Dios,"* she whispered. Maybe the cross really would do Nellie some good. Nellie had taken it as a sign of friendship, and Jeanmarie felt glad to think of her wearing it. The poor woman had little enough and maybe no real friends.

Jeanmarie sighed deeply. Her own heart was breaking for her friend Wilfred, and if he died, how could she bear it? For a long time she tossed and turned. Hot and tired, she sat up, wondering if Pearl was asleep. She got up quietly, slipped into the deserted hallway, and took the elevator upstairs.

"Pearl, it's me, Jeanmarie," she whispered softly, standing by Pearl's bed.

"Hey, what are you doing here?" Pearl asked, sitting up.

"Couldn't sleep. I thought you might want company too," Jeanmarie said. "Can you move over? All I need is a little room."

Pearl pushed over to one side of the bed. "Hop in," she whispered. Back at the orphanage on cold nights most of the girls doubled their blankets by sharing their iron cots, and the two of them were used to small spaces.

"I keep thinking about Wilfred," Jeanmarie said, lying on her good side facing Pearl.

"Me too." Pearl's voice ended with a sigh.

"He told me once that he never knew who his father or mother were," Jeanmarie said. She choked back a sob. Pearl sighed deeply as she reached for Jeanmarie's hand and held it. After a while she began to think and the tears stopped. "Wilfred's folks must have been brilliant to have Wilfred. I think one day he'll be president of something, maybe a big company," she said.

"Or even superintendent of Apple Valley Orphanage," Pearl whispered. "I doubt Dr. Werner would like that much. I'm sure he plans on being superintendent forever."

Jeanmarie thought about Dr. Werner for a moment. "Do you think they called him about Wilfred? He might show up here tomorrow." The idea made her groan. "How will we ever explain what happened? For instance there's Nellie."

"Who's Nellie?" Pearl asked.

"It's a long story," she began. By the time she'd finished she could hardly keep her eyes open. "I think I can sleep now," she said.

"Poor Nellie," Pearl said. A light snore followed her words, and Jeanmarie knew she was asleep.

A deep sadness touched Jeanmarie. She hated the thought of Nellie locked in that terrible place upstairs. She didn't want to think of Wilfred, lying hurt and broken either. Pearl sighed in her sleep. And worst of all, Jeanmarie was afraid for Pearl. What if her eyes didn't heal? She pictured Pearl, her head bowed and a white cane in her hand to help her walk. There were places where blind people went to school. Would that happen to Pearl? How could they be best friends with Pearl blind and far away? "Stop it," she told herself. Nothing like that was going to happen.

Out of nowhere, Nellie's words came to her mind: "Will you be my friend?" Poor Nellie. What would it be like to have no friends?

The next thing Jeanmarie knew she heard the sounds of rattling carts. She stretched. Pearl mumbled something about morning. "I better get out of here and back downstairs," Jeanmarie said. "Thanks for the company, and don't worry, I'll be back as soon as visiting hours come."

"Mm, okay," Pearl murmured.

In the corridor staff were already moving about, but nobody paid any attention to Jeanmarie. "Guess I look like one of their patients," she thought. The staff were too busy to care. Luckily there were no nurses in the hallway as she waited for the elevator. Safely inside she pressed the button for her floor and drew in a sharp breath. It worked. But would she ever stop thinking "Nellie" every time she took the elevator?

FIFTEEN

A Point of Light

*T*he broad-shouldered doctor had finished listening to Jeanmarie's heart. He poked the area around her appendectomy wound once more. "Good, good," he said. "So, lass, I hear you've been exploring our grand Bellevue Hospital, a bit of a dangerous thing to do. And what were you thinking you'd find down in all those old rooms? No dungeons or the like, I hope."

Jeanmarie smiled at the doctor. "No dungeons," she said, "just an old chapel."

"Aye, and that's worth the seeing," he agreed. "Well, for all your adventures you're in good shape, and I think you ought to be going on home by the weekend. Once we get those stitches out you can rest as well at home. We'd better not keep her too long, right, nurse? She just might be off exploring again and get herself lost for good." He leaned toward Jeanmarie confidentially. "Every school term we lose a young student or two in this place. So remember, lass, no more exploring, and in a few weeks you'll be good as new." He stood, smiled, and walked quickly on to the next patient, with his troop of interns following behind. Jeanmarie didn't see the tall figure striding toward her.

"Exploring, was it?" Jeanmarie felt her stomach drop. Dr. Werner stood towering above her, his dark suit matching the frown on his face. "Perhaps, young lady, you can fill me in on some of the details concerning Wilfred's accident," he said. "I am a bit vague on what you were all doing down in the subterranean parts of the old hospital."

"Oh," Jeanmarie said, not knowing what to say next. "Poor Wilfred. Is he improving?" She looked at Dr. Werner hopefully.

Dr. Werner stood stiff and tall. "Wilfred is a fortunate lad. Indeed, fortunate. As far as we know his lungs are functioning well, and there appears to be no puncture from the broken ribs. He is, of course, very weak from his ordeal. Both arms are in casts, and one shoulder." Dr. Werner wiped his forehead with a spotless white handkerchief, folded it, and returned it to his pocket. "Wilfred is resting and will be convalescing for some time to come. We must be thankful once again for the care of Providence."

"I'm truly thankful," Jeanmarie managed to say. She tried to swallow past the lump in her throat. Dr. Werner's stern look had returned, and she knew he expected a full confession.

"And I am truly waiting for your explanations, Miss. Exactly why were the three of you wandering about? Surely, I thought one might rest easy knowing you had just had an appendectomy, but I find that I was wrong to assume your natural capacity for getting into trouble somehow left you in the operating room. You may proceed." He moved to the edge of Jeanmarie's bed. "I believe I shall sit down for this. May I?"

Jeanmarie nodded emphatically. "Well, you remember the day of the fire?" she began.

"All too well," Dr. Werner said quietly.

"It all began then," Jeanmarie continued. When she had finished telling all except the part about being locked up with Nellie, she stopped and sat silently waiting. Not for all the world would she mention Nellie. Dr. Werner already considered her wild enough, but so far he'd kept her at the orphanage. Her throat felt dry as she waited.

Dr. Werner cleared his throat. "Did it ever occur to you to tell someone in authority that this Slavko might be hiding in the basement? Instead you acted on impulse and took it upon yourself to organize a manhunt for a thief."

Jeanmarie gulped. Impulse. It was one of her worst faults.

"It was *your* plan?" Dr. Werner demanded.

Jeanmarie's face burned. She'd wanted Wilfred to go along even before he suggested looking at the old chapel, so it really was her plan. "Yes, sir," she said.

"I cannot hold you responsible for Wilfred's decision to accompany you or for his insatiable thirst for knowledge that led him to explore further on his own, but I do hold you responsible for your own actions." Dr. Werner's voice grew sterner. "And for that matter I believe you provided for Pearl to accompany you and Wilfred?"

Jeanmarie nodded her head, heavy with misery. "Yes, and I know it was my fault that Wilfred got hurt," she said in a small voice.

Dr. Werner lifted her chin with his finger. "Look at me. And do not forget what I am about to say. Wilfred is a young man totally capable of making his own decisions. You are not responsible for his accident." He loosed her chin. "None of us wish Wilfred had fallen in that hole," he said. "But it wouldn't have happened if he had not decided to explore on his own. Perhaps he would not have gone to the basement without your plan, but I know that Wilfred desperately wanted to see the old rooms and the old chapels for himself. Unfortunately, I myself gave him a short history of Bellevue." Dr. Werner cleared his throat again. "Now, I do not believe I am responsible for his accident, and neither should you."

"Yes, sir." Jeanmarie stifled a smile at the thought that maybe Dr. Werner was at least a little guilty for giving Wilfred that book knowing Wilfred's weakness for learning.

Dr. Werner stood. "The doctor says you and Pearl may return to the orphanage on Friday. I shall come for you at precisely 2:00, Friday afternoon." Unsmiling, he said, "Must I remind you that I expect no more wandering off? See that you stay out of trouble for the next few days. That is an order."

"Yes, sir," Jeanmarie said, relief flooding over her like a cool breeze. He'd said nothing about punishment. She watched him leave. On the other hand, he might be waiting until they were back at the orphanage. She glanced at the clock on the wall, still three whole hours until visiting hours. Would they let her visit Wilfred? He would probably be asleep most of the day anyway. What about Pearl? Did she know they were going home Friday? She couldn't wait until visiting hours to find out.

Upstairs in an examining room Pearl sat stiffly in a padded chair while a doctor undid the bandages from her eyes. "I want you to keep your eyes closed until I tell you to open them, and then open them slowly," he said. "You may see a little, maybe nothing yet; but we have to find out what's going on here."

The nurse holding Pearl's hand squeezed it. "Okay," Pearl whispered. She closed her eyes.

"I'm taking the last of the bandage off now," the doctor said. "Slowly, slowly open your eyes."

Pearl opened her eyes, blinked, and blinked again. She snatched her hand from the nurse's and felt her eyes with her fingers. They were open. "I don't see anything but a tiny point of light. Why can't I see?" She half rose from the chair, and the nurse gently pressed her shoulder.

The doctor cleared his throat. "Now, Pearl," he said, "this may be only a temporary state. Sometimes a blow on the head like the one you suffered will cause a problem with sight, but we don't know that yet. There is also a kind of stress-induced blindness that can be temporary. You have been through a lot of stress in that circus fire. Your eyes certainly suffered a great deal of irritation from the smoke." He lifted Pearl's chin and peered into her eyes. "Do you see shadows or only that point of light?"

"Just the dot, but not in one place. It seems to move sometimes," she said.

The doctor patted her arm. "Well, young lady, I think the best thing we can do is give your eyes time. I'd like to see you again in three weeks. Unless of course there is any change. If you have headaches or pressure or anything unusual you must have Dr. Werner contact me right away. I'll have a word with him so he knows what we're looking for." The doctor took Pearl's hand in his. "Yours isn't the first case where nothing obvious seems to have caused the loss of sight, and the cure can come just as mysteriously." He touched her head lightly where the abrasion had been. "No swelling, and it has healed nicely. Now we could take a look inside and see if we're missing something here, but my best advice is that we wait and see what a few weeks' rest does. Any questions? If not, the nurse will take you back to your room."

"No questions," Pearl said quietly.

The doctor patted her arm. "That's the girl."

"Please," Pearl said. "When can I go home?"

"You mean the orphanage?" the doctor said. "I don't see any reason why you should stay past the weekend, and I've already spoken by phone to Dr. Werner. However, I'd like for Dr. Schwartz to take a look at your eyes before you leave, just to confirm my opinion. He'll be back Friday morning, and you can go home the same day. The nurse will schedule your appointment with Dr. Schwartz. Be good," he said as the nurse wheeled her out.

When Jeanmarie arrived she found Pearl sitting in the chair by the bed. "It's me," she said. "Dr. Werner just came by to say he's coming back this Friday for us. Have you heard already?"

"Yes, I can leave Friday," Pearl said in a low voice.

"I'll be glad to go. How about you?" Pearl was silent. Jeanmarie sat on the edge of the bed close to her chair. "What's happened?" she asked.

"They took the bandages off this morning," Pearl said quietly.

"But you still have them on. That's it—oh no, it can't be." Jeanmarie wrung her hands.

"It is; it is. I can't see, and that's the end of it. I may never see again. They might have to operate to look inside if my eyes don't heal by themselves." Pearl's voice sounded flat, hopeless to Jeanmarie.

Jeanmarie knelt on the floor and grasped Pearl's hands. "What do you mean when you say *if* your eyes don't heal by themselves?" she asked.

"The doctor said sometimes no one knows what causes the blindness or what brings the eyesight back; it just happens. But he didn't promise it would happen. He said I'm to go back in three weeks unless something changes." Her voice began to rise. "I can't see; don't you get it? Not now and maybe never."

Jeanmarie ignored the anger and wrapped her arms around Pearl, holding her tight. "We're going home together, this Friday. I'll be there with you; all of us will."

"I know," Pearl wailed. "I just want to see again. How will I get around? It's summer, and I won't be able to swim or read or anything."

Jeanmarie laughed through her tears. "We'll make it together," she said. "I'll be your eyes, and you can be the brains for both of us. At least it *is* summer. We can go for walks, and I can read to you. And like Chaplain Stone would say, pray." She saw a little smile on Pearl's face. Chaplain Stone, not really a chaplain but an FBI agent, had become a hero to both of them. "It's going to be alright. It can happen just like the doctor said."

"Three weeks is so long to wait," Pearl said.

"We'll do it together, remember?" Jeanmarie's heart was breaking, but she wouldn't let it for Pearl's sake. "And if I'm not on restrictions for the rest of the month we can listen to the radio, every program we like!" Werner might put her on restrictions for the rest of the year, but she could hope. She wiped her eyes and stood. "Listen, if we're leaving on Friday, we should say good-bye to the princess, shouldn't we?" she said. The thought had just occurred to her.

Pearl brushed a strand of hair from her face. "I guess we should," she said.

"We can go together. You know where her room is, and I don't. You do know, don't you?" As Pearl shook her head, Jeanmarie groaned. "Don't say it. It's somewhere on the other side of the big tunnel."

"I didn't say it, you did," Pearl said. "But if you think I'm going all over this hospital looking for a tunnel so we can both get lost, no way."

"Okay, so no tunnel. Maybe we could send her a note," Jeanmarie suggested. She smiled. Pearl sounded more like her old self.

"One problem," Pearl said. "We can't send it to 'the princess' or 'Maya from the circus' without any room number or last name." She laughed. "How about 'The Beautiful Lady'?"

"Why, that would do nicely," said a voice from the doorway. Jeanmarie whirled around and saw the princess standing there. She was wearing a soft blue summer dress with lace at the sleeves and a matching blue straw hat banded with small yellow flowers. "I only have a minute, my dears," she said. "The car is waiting for me, and I promised Willie I would hurry. I just came to say good-bye."

She hugged them both. "I shall think of you often. When you come to the circus again you must visit me. And don't worry about Slavko. The police are satisfied, and there won't be any charges. He has promised to return home and behave himself. I really must go," she said. Jeanmarie and Pearl waited with her until the elevator came.

Pearl heard the door close. "I know this sounds strange," she said softly, "but if angels are ever people for a while I think the princess could be one. When she came to see me that night, she said I could learn to use my whole body, all the gifts God gave me, even if I couldn't see. And I was starting to learn, beginning to hear and feel, sort of like with my

123

whole body." Pearl gripped Jeanmarie's arm. "It was like a game then. Only when they took off the bandages this morning I forgot everything. I couldn't see, and nothing else mattered." Pearl's voice grew wistful. "I know the princess is right. It's not the end of life when something like that happens, but I'm just not ready." She found Jeanmarie's hand and held it.

Jeanmarie swallowed hard. "Don't think like that," she said. "You can't give in; it isn't right. Don't let yourself think anything else." Her grip tightened on Pearl's hand.

"Lunchtime," a nurse announced, setting a metal tray next to Pearl's bed. She looked sternly at Jeanmarie. "Now, you know visiting hours haven't started yet. You better go along back to your room and let this young woman eat her lunch." She turned to Pearl. "Until you are officially dismissed you are still my patient. So eat up. And you, girl, run along now."

Jeanmarie left quietly. Her own lunch was probably waiting for her back in the ward. As she went she felt the heavy weight of Pearl's words. She didn't want her to be noble. She hated the thought of Pearl never seeing again. She must never let her think that way again. Pearl *had* to see for both their sakes.

SIXTEEN

Doctor's Orders

*T*he lunch of soup, bread, and a kind of lemon pudding
sat on a tray next to Jeanmarie's bed. While she ate, Jeanmarie thought about the orphanage; she pictured Winnie
and the others at the small tables in the large dining room
laughing and chattering. Having lunch here in the ward full
of patients felt different—lonely, in spite of the noise of trays
and patients. A nurse in a green uniform across the ward
caught her attention. She was coming toward Jeanmarie
and smiling at her. In a moment recognition flooded over
Jeanmarie: the nurse from the operating room! "Aren't
you the one who brought me the cross?" she asked.

"Right, that's me. And don't ask me how it ended
up on Nellie Gray's neck, but here it is again. I knew
it was yours." The nurse turned the cross over and
pointed to the initials M. G. "They stand for Maria
Gonzalez, the girl who left it to you."

For a second Jeanmarie felt numb. "You don't mean Nellie the woman from upstairs died? But how?"

"Oh dear, she isn't dead," the nurse said quickly. "Just broke her hip falling off a ladder in the supply closet on one of her escapes from the psych ward."

"The supply closet?"

"That's right, and what on earth she was doing in there, we'll never know." The nurse laid the cross on Jeanmarie's bed. "Nellie must have picked it up in the washroom or the hallway on one of her wanderings. When it comes to getting loose, Nellie is the best. She won't be going anywhere for the next few weeks with a broken hip. Poor thing." The nurse looked at her watch. "Lunch break; I better get going."

Jeanmarie didn't know what to say. She knew she couldn't explain how Nellie really got the cross. "Thanks, but maybe she ought to keep it. I don't mind." She held the cross out.

"Honey, Nellie won't even remember she found it, and it belongs to you. Got to go."

Jeanmarie still held the cross on her palm, but it was too late, the nurse had gone. Reluctantly she put it around her neck. Would Nellie remember? At least Nellie's secret was still safe. Only Pearl knew about it. She had told Wilfred about the first time she'd met Nellie on the elevator, but that was all. Wilfred—how could she have forgotten Wilfred? Jeanmarie shook her head. "Dunce," she said to herself. "Why didn't I ask the nurse from the operating room about him when she was right here!"

An elderly woman who handled the patients' mail interrupted Jeanmarie's thoughts as she handed her a large brown envelope. "Must be a big card in there, dearie," she said, winking at Jeanmarie. The return address said Apple Valley Orphanage. Carefully Jeanmarie opened it. The two youngest orphans in Wheelock Cottage, Lizzie and May, had drawn pictures, one of the yard behind Wheelock and the other showing the two little girls at the swimming hole. She smiled, thinking of them. Motherless Lizzie called her "my Jean-marie-Nanny." The letter folded inside was from Winnie and addressed to both her and Pearl. She read it quickly and turned it over. "So you see, all of us, including Lizzie and May, can hardly wait until you get here," Winnie wrote. "And one thing more, Mrs. Ripple's older sister had an operation on her leg. Mrs. R. is taking the rest of the month off to help her out. You will never guess who is coming to replace her—Matron!"

Jeanmarie groaned and looked away from the letter in her hand. Mrs. Ripple would have helped Pearl. But of all the substitute housemothers in the world, Miss Grundy, or Matron, as Winnie and the rest of the girls at Wheelock Cottage called her, was the worst. The woman had substituted for a whole month once before, and they'd all hoped never to see her again. Matron might be only a nickname, but it fit. She did things at Wheelock as if she were running a jail or correctional institute instead of an orphanage. How could Dr. Werner do this to them?

Winnie's last few lines brought a brief smile to Jeanmarie. "The twins and I are planning a welcome party even the Matron won't be able to stop." That would take some doing, she thought. She slipped the letter and the pictures back into the envelope. Poor Pearl. Why couldn't it have been Miss Grundy's sister who broke a leg? Matron meant only trouble for all of them.

Friday came quickly. Dressed in her own clothes, Jeanmarie marveled at how loosely they hung on her, except where the bandage on her side raised a large, obvious lump.

Even her legs looked skinny to her. But at least she could walk now without bending over. As a young nurse's aide wheeled Pearl to the entryway of the ward, Jeanmarie swallowed hard. Pearl too had on the same clothes she'd worn the day of the circus and fresh, white bandages around her eyes.

"You and your friend here can wait together for your ride home," the aide said. She parked the wheelchair and set the brake. "You just sit right here now 'til your ride comes. It's so busy, I got patients waiting in line upstairs. Now you all stay well, you hear?"

The smells of food brought in by visitors and the noise of people all talking at once filled the ward. Pearl chuckled and said, "So you didn't have a private room? I guess you'll miss all this."

"If cows can fly," Jeanmarie said. At precisely 2:00 Dr. Werner arrived, dressed as usual in a black suit. "Here he comes," she whispered.

Dr. Werner smiled. "Well now, you will be glad to hear Wilfred is recovering, coming along nicely, and I have signed the two of you out," he said. "Is there anything you need before we leave? If not, I shall call for an aide and another chair for you, Jeanmarie, and we will be on our way. Hospital rules, you understand. All postoperative patients must be wheeled to the car. Wait here." He strode quickly to the nurses' station.

Jeanmarie sighed. It didn't matter that she could walk fine; Dr. Werner thought of rules as sacred, never to be broken. She touched Pearl's shoulder. "If only Weary Willie would show up now. Dr. Werner needs a good dose of Willie, don't you think?" she whispered. Pearl giggled.

With a last glance at the massive stone hospital where so much had happened in such a little while, Jeanmarie settled next to Pearl in the backseat of Dr. Werner's car. She would never forget Bellevue. On the car radio station Frank Sinatra was singing "Those Golden Earrings," one of her favorite songs. It reminded her that she hadn't heard a radio for days. As the station switched to news, she remembered something else—she'd almost forgotten the war!

"London has been the main target of the German flying bombs since June 15," the announcer said. "Prime Minister Churchill disclosed that since that date the enemy has sent over 2,754 missiles. Those that landed killed 2,752 persons, an average of one human being per bomb launched—and gravely injured 8,000 others."

Jeanmarie touched Pearl's arm. "So many people in less than a month?" Her mind couldn't grasp the terrible picture as she listened.

The announcer's voice was grim. "Mr. Churchill saw little hope of an early end to the menace," he said. "He believes even heavier rockets might strike Britain . . . children are being evacuated from London and the city's deep shelters will soon be opened to the public."

Without comment Dr. Werner switched the station to music. "I have a few things to say before we reach the orphanage," he said. He cleared his throat. "Ahem. Now, you may not realize that while Bellevue Hospital is indeed an old establishment and the world's largest city hospital, the reputation of Bellevue's doctors is excellent. I have no doubt that they will do everything possible for you, Pearl, and we shall expect good results. And you know that we will return for your checkup in three weeks. I am sure you will have all the help you need getting around until then." He cleared his throat once more. "As for you, Jeanmarie, I expect you to stay out of trouble. You will report to the school nurse in a week's time, and we shall see how you are progressing. The doctor assures me you are doing fine. I only wish I were as certain of your conduct."

Jeanmarie could feel sweat running down her neck. She wished Dr. Werner would just tell her what punishment he had decided on. Pearl reached for her hand and squeezed it.

"However," Dr. Werner continued, "I am expecting you to follow all the doctor's orders, young lady. You do recall them—no lifting, no strenuous physical exertion for the next three weeks, and that includes swimming, running, climbing, and the like?"

"Yes, sir," Jeanmarie replied.

"Well then, we shall see. I assume you will undertake to serve as a companion for Pearl while you both recover. She will, of course, need a guide and helping hand. And you will cooperate fully with Miss Grundy, who is standing in for Mrs. Ripple until the end of the month."

Jeanmarie could barely control her voice, "Oh yes, sir."

As the car pulled up in front of Wheelock Cottage, a cheer broke out. All the girls were lined up on the steps of the porch, and Lizzie and May were holding up cardboard signs that said "Welcome Home." Above them in the doorway, her face solemn, her arms folded, stood Matron.

SEVENTEEN

Friends Forever

Jeanmarie waved at the little group waiting in front of Wheelock. Behind them the old stone building entwined with dark ivy vines looked mellow under the July sun and cloudless blue sky. She glanced quickly toward the woods where thick plots of wild phlox bloomed purple and white and at the small birds darting among the maple trees in full greenery, all of it home to her.

"Here we go; step up," Dr. Werner instructed Pearl, his hand under her elbow. Pearl felt for the next step and stumbled. Dr. Werner's strong grip kept her upright. "Careful now," he cautioned. "Try feeling with your foot for the back of the step and then let your other foot find the top of the next one. Good." Behind them Jeanmarie and the others watched silently.

Inside, Dr. Werner presented Pearl to Miss Grundy. "I will leave the girls in your capable hands," he said. "I have asked Jeanmarie to act as Pearl's companion and helper. If you have any questions I shall be in my office. I believe you have the school nurse's schedule should you need to call her."

Miss Grundy continued frowning. "Well, we'll see how it goes," she said, adding as Dr. Werner left, "Here, girl, you hold on to her," and placing Pearl's hand in Jeanmarie's. Pointing to the door she said, "The rest of you girls stay quiet outdoors where I can see you." Jeanmarie saw Winnie frown as she shepherded a reluctant Lizzie and May outside. The others followed silently.

Miss Grundy, with her hands on her hips and a scowl on her face, surveyed Pearl and Jeanmarie. "So one of you's just getting over an operation and the other's blind. Seems to me that's a miserable combination." Jeanmarie flinched at the word *blind*. Miss Grundy added more, her words pouring out like bitter water. "It don't make sense mixing blind folks in with seeing ones when there's them paid to handle this kind of trouble. Nothing like this in the rules that goes with this job. They got special schools and such for that sort of thing. Guess I have to make do with it for now." She sat down heavily on a kitchen chair. "Suppose you can set up meals in the kitchen. Won't be so messy in the dining room that way." Not once had she addressed Pearl or uttered a word of sympathy.

Jeanmarie felt her face grow warm. At her side Pearl trembled. "You won't have to worry about meals," Jeanmarie said. "Pearl and I don't mind eating in the kitchen, do we?"

"Fine, just fine," Pearl mumbled.

Miss Grundy looked at her and nodded. "I 'spect it's best, then. It appears to me you got yourself a full-time job here, Missy." Her hard eyes looked at Jeanmarie. "You'll have to watch out for the stairs, see to the bath, and help her do just about everything that needs doing."

"I don't mind, really," Jeanmarie insisted. She didn't trust herself to say more. The woman acted as if Pearl wasn't even there! Her throat ached with holding back angry words, but it wouldn't do any good to say them and might get them both in trouble. Pearl said nothing.

"Better get along upstairs then and change your clothes and hers. You can rest on your beds until supper time. I don't want you going up and down stairs more than needed. You come down in the morning and stay down, except of course for using the bathroom. Tomorrow you can sit on chairs and snap beans, make yourself useful." Miss Grundy motioned Jeanmarie toward the kitchen door. "One thing more," she called after them, "I ain't gonna be responsible for any accidents around here. I suppose the orphanage didn't want to spend the money for your proper care, but that don't make it right. You ought to be where they make it easy for folks like you, girl. So don't you go walking around by yourself, understand?"

Jeanmarie felt Pearl stiffen. "Right," Pearl said, her lips rigid.

Jeanmarie held Pearl's thin arm tightly and walked her quickly out of the kitchen into the hallway away from Miss Grundy. "She doesn't belong here," Jeanmarie said. Mrs. Ripple would have welcomed them both with some cheer. She patted Pearl's arm. "Don't let her get to you. The woman has a mean streak a yard wide. She hasn't changed since the last time she was here."

Pearl bit her lip. When she spoke her voice fell flat and dull. "You won't have to help me do everything. I can take care of myself mostly, once I know where things are. I suppose she's right; the orphanage didn't want to spend the money to put me someplace for the blind." Pearl turned her head toward Jeanmarie. "They'll have to, you know, once they find I'm blind for good."

Jeanmarie felt herself trembling. "Don't say that," she pleaded. "No one is going to put you anywhere. In three weeks the bandages will come off and you'll be fine. I know it in my heart. As for Grundy, we'll just stay out of her way." They had come to the stairway leading upstairs. Jeanmarie stopped and put Pearl's hand on the banister.

"Wait a minute," she said. "Remember how many times you've been up and down this staircase? Can you picture it in your mind?" This had to work. "Think of the wall to your left going up, the banister on your right. Remember the steps are wooden, and some of them squeak. How big are they? How many are there?"

Pearl concentrated. "I see it in my mind, but I don't know how many steps there are. A lot."

"Okay," Jeanmarie agreed, "but it's our old staircase, and you know it well enough to go up it in the dark if you had to. I'm closing my eyes tightly and I'm going up first. When I reach the top I'll wait for you. So here we go." With her hand on the rail in front of Pearl's hand she closed her eyes deliberately and felt for the first step and then the next until there were no more steps. At the top Jeanmarie opened her eyes and stood aside. "You can do it," she called softly. Pearl had already begun climbing. At the top Jeanmarie helped her feel where the railing ended and the wall turned a corner. "You did it," she said. "And next time we'll count them."

"Hold up a minute," Pearl pleaded. "I'm seeing where we are. If I go along this wall," she felt the wall on her right, "I should come to the door to the little girls' dorm. Past that door the wall goes on until it turns left, and then there's the small bathroom. After that, the wall turns left again straight to our dorm!"

"You have it!" Jeanmarie cried. "Do you want to try?"

"Yes, but this time maybe you should keep your eyes open just in case," Pearl said.

A surge of pride filled Jeanmarie as she watched Pearl slowly but surely finding her way. "It's working," she called to her.

In the doorway of their dorm, Pearl stood and waited. "This has to be our dorm, but here's where the wall ends and the maze begins." It was clear what she meant. Except for part of the wall to the left with its closet and dressers, the other three walls with the fire escape door on one side, and the two large windows on another, were a maze of iron cots sticking out in several directions. Some were full length against a wall, others with only the head of the bed against it. It was one thing to feel a wall, another to cross empty space to the iron cots.

Jeanmarie guided Pearl to her own bed and let her sit. "The place is full of iron waiting to bang your shins. We'll think of something," she said. She closed her eyes and tried to imagine the room and shook her head. "I don't suppose we could move the beds?"

The party late that night in the corner of the dorm by the fire escape door went smoothly. Jeanmarie didn't ask where the refreshments had come from. She didn't need to ask about the green apples, tart and wonderful. The meadow was full of them. The girls were listening to Winnie's idea. "So," Winnie whispered, "we could make a kind of guide rope from the door handle to the dresser knobs past the closet, tie it to the foot of the first bed, then on to the foot of the next

135

one, straight around the room and back to Maria's bed by the doorway."

It sounded so simple, but it was perfect. Jeanmarie whispered back, "Win, you're right. And if each of us contributes a scarf, a belt, whatever we can find, it should work. We'll do it first thing in the morning."

"Too bad we couldn't do the whole house that way," Winnie said, "but Matron would never bend that much."

She hadn't bent at all. By mid-morning all the guide rope was taken down. "Nonsense, and an accident waiting to happen," Miss Grundy said. "I'll have no more of this sort of thing. Another incident like this and we'll see about some changes here."

Jeanmarie squeezed Pearl's hand. Under her breath she muttered, "Someone should change *her.*" Whatever Miss Grundy meant by changes, the threat behind her words hung in the air like a cloud full of menace.

Eating in the kitchen at least meant they were out of Grundy's watchful eye, though Pearl seemed to have little appetite. Jeanmarie studied Pearl's face, pale under the freckles below the bandages. She wasn't sleeping well either. Twice she'd fallen over things left on the floor, things as simple as a forgotten pair of shoes. Miss Grundy made things worse. Daily she complained over little things Pearl did unknowingly like snapping too much off the ends of the string beans, dropping things, bumping into things. Jeanmarie and Pearl were no longer allowed outdoors with the others but had to wait until everyone else had gone to the man-made orphanage swimming hole for recreation time. If Miss Grundy had her way, most of the day Pearl would sit on a chair doing small chores or just sit quietly.

"Let me get us more pudding," Jeanmarie offered. "It's the only thing you've eaten, and I know there's extra."

Pearl said listlessly, "At least it stays on the spoon."

"Good, then I'll be back in a minute. Winnie and Maria never eat butterscotch pudding. They'll be glad to get rid of it." Jeanmarie hurried into the dining room. She had just stopped to talk for a minute when the loud sound of something crashing in the kitchen brought her heart to her mouth. She ran, but Miss Grundy was already standing in the kitchen entry, hands on her hips. On the floor by the sink broken dishes lay scattered.

Pearl stood holding onto the edge of the sink. "I'm sorry," she said. "I must have knocked some dishes over when I tried to put our plates into the sink. I am so sorry."

"Well, why didn't you just wait for somebody to take care of the plates, Miss? You can't see what you've done, but it's one big mess," Miss Grundy said loudly. "I don't get paid for this, you know," she added.

Red spots appeared in Pearl's cheeks. With one hand she searched for the countertop, her fingers feeling across a tray of dirty dishes. A cup tumbled over, and she drew back her hand with a cry. Jeanmarie ran to her.

"That's it!" Miss Grundy screeched. "You take that girl out of here and see her upstairs to her bed. And the two of you stay there. I knew something like this would happen."

Upstairs, Jeanmarie tried to comfort Pearl. "I've tried; I have," Pearl said between sobs. "What if I can only see a little or not at all when they take the bandages off the next time? Dr. Werner will never let me stay now. I don't want to go to some institute for the blind. And I've done my best; it's just not good enough."

"Nothing anybody does is good enough for Matron," Jeanmarie said. "Nothing pleases that woman. Don't worry, Mrs.

Ripple will be back here in just two more weeks. She won't let them take you." Mrs. Ripple was fair, at least, and Pearl's blindness wouldn't trouble her. Not much troubled Mrs. Ripple. Jeanmarie smoothed Pearl's hair from her forehead. "I shouldn't have left you alone. From now on consider me your shadow." Pearl wiped her face with the edge of one sleeve. Her thin arm looked thinner than ever. Jeanmarie frowned. "One thing," she said, "you have to promise you'll try to eat more, or nobody will know which one of us is the shadow."

A small smile appeared at Pearl's mouth for a second. "I will, if you'll promise me something," she said.

"Done," Jeanmarie said. She had no idea what Pearl wanted, but whatever it was she'd do it to see her eat again.

"Swear to me, that no matter what happens, you won't forget me. If they take me away, promise you'll write; even if I can't read I'll know it's from you, and I'll keep it until I find a way. You and the others are all I have in the world." Pearl reached for Jeanmarie's hand and held it.

"Pearl"—Jeanmarie swallowed hard to speak—"no matter where you are or where I am, true friends are forever. Friends stick by each other. It's what friends do." The words echoed in her mind; someone else had said the same thing— Nellie!

EIGHTEEN

"Vaya con Dios"

Jeanmarie let the light breeze from the dorm window play on her face. Three days without a single accident! She brushed the hair from her eyes and wiped away the sweat running down her face. She'd run outside to make sure Miss Grundy was truly gone. By this time the housemother was safely in Ford Cottage high on the hill for an afternoon tea with the other housemothers. Girls' recreation at the swimming hole always took a whole afternoon, leaving the women free to visit once a week. Jeanmarie smiled. It meant an afternoon of freedom for Pearl and herself, and it wouldn't include sitting outside on two kitchen chairs until Grundy came home, at least not until the last minute.

Slowly feeling her way, Pearl moved along the upstairs hallway. Pride flooded Jeanmarie as she watched. Pearl could do so much on her own when Matron wasn't around to keep her from trying. At the doorway Pearl called, "Ready?"

"Ready," Jeanmarie echoed. "Grundy is gone and won't be back for hours." Pearl didn't wait for her and was already making her own way down the stairs. At the bottom she turned and headed to the kitchen, stepped inside, and felt her way along the wall until it turned, past the laundry tubs, and then to the kitchen door. She stood waiting with a triumphant smile on her face.

Behind her Jeanmarie clapped lightly. "Pearl, Princess couldn't have done better. She'd be proud of you." Linking her arm in Pearl's she counted down the porch steps until they reached level ground. "Now the whole world is ours. Want to walk along the road toward town? We can follow the tracks for a while. You can smell the honeysuckle growing alongside them. Just listen to those birds. Feel the sun on your face?"

Pearl laughed. "Slow down." She lifted her face to the sun. "It does feel wonderful. The breeze is just enough, and I can't wait to smell the honeysuckle. Lead on," she commanded. Sliding a little on the grassy bank down to the tracks Pearl had slipped and landed on her bottom, laughing. "It feels so good to be me again," she said. "Let's sit here and just listen."

They'd sat, listening, talking some when Jeanmarie tapped Pearl's arm. "Hear that buzz?" she asked. "A fat bumblebee wants us out of here." Pearl flew to her feet as Jeanmarie knew she would.

Every summer they'd walked the forbidden railroad tracks, but this time it was different. Pearl stumbled and clutched her arm. "Stupid of me," Jeanmarie said. "Sorry, but I think walking the tracks is too hard."

"No, wait," Pearl insisted. "If I can just get the hang of it, I can do it." A minute later she fell forward too quickly for Jeanmarie to save her. Struggling to get up she cried out, "My foot is caught! I can't get it loose!"

"Let me try," Jeanmarie said, kneeling by her. "Your shoe is wedged tight. I'll have to find a stick or something to pry you out."

"Ugh," Pearl said. "Don't go far, will you? I hope there isn't a train on its way." She pulled at her leg with both hands. "I'm really stuck."

Jeanmarie found a thick, heavy stick the size she wanted. "Let's try this," she said. It took all her strength, but it worked. "You okay?"

Pearl rubbed her foot and felt around the shoe. "I think so; thanks."

"We'd better get off these tracks and back on the road. Your foot is starting to swell, and it looks bruised." Jeanmarie helped Pearl up and guided her off the tracks.

Pearl limped along, her shoe in her hand. "I can't let Grundy find out about this or we'll both be in trouble."

"I'll put some ice on that foot as soon as we get back," Jeanmarie promised. "You can wear my white socks and sandals, and I'll wear your shoes. These old sandals are so stretched out one of our cows could wear them." Pearl, still limping, responded with a "humph."

The silence of the house brought a sigh of relief from Pearl. "Nobody's home, thankfully," she said. Minutes later Jeanmarie slipped ice wrapped in a napkin inside the loose, white sock on Pearl's bruised foot. "It feels wonderful," Pearl said; "the sandals too." Half an hour later she managed to stand and walk without limping, or barely so.

"Jeanmarie, even Grundy can't deny us some cold tea. I'm dying for it, and I insist you let me make it. I promise, no broken dishes this time." Pearl felt her way along the kitchen from table to stove and picked up the kettle from the back burner. "I've gone over this kitchen in my mind a hundred times, picturing every inch of it," Pearl said. "I think I could make a meal, with a little help."

Jeanmarie laughed and clapped her hands. "Pearl, I know you could. There isn't anything you can't do, or most anything, once you've made up your mind."

Pearl sloshed the water in the kettle. "Sounds like enough to me. I'll put the kettle on if you'll get the tea and the ice. Tea's on the first shelf in the cupboard near the laundry."

Forgetting, Jeanmarie nodded and quickly caught herself. "Right," she said.

Pearl felt the back burner. It was far too cool to boil water. She'd have to add a few coals and rouse the fire a bit. The coal bucket sat next to the stove where it always sat, and she felt for the small hand shovel on top, found it, and soon added her coal. "There we go; that will heat up quickly." She'd found a pot holder and pushed the burner lid back in place. Something stung at her hand, and she slapped at it.

Jeanmarie turned and screamed, "Pearl, the pot holder is on fire!" She ran to the stove and quickly poured water from the kettle over the burning cloth. Pearl's face was a deathly white. "It's okay!" Jeanmarie cried. "The fire is out, and everything is all right."

From the doorway a hard voice demanded, "Fire, what fire? What's going on here?" Miss Grundy strode to the stove and with hands on her hips glared at both girls. "This does it. Out of this kitchen, into the parlor, and don't move from the sofa until I say so. Lucky I came back early. I'm phoning Dr. Werner at once."

An hour later, left to themselves in the empty parlor, Pearl whispered, "It's over." Dr. Werner had come and gone, promising Miss Grundy to locate a place for Pearl as soon as possible. "At least temporarily," he'd said to Pearl, "while your bandages are still on." He said nothing to Jeanmarie, but the shake of his head and the grim "I knew it" look on his face as he left had been enough. Shame flooded her, burning her face. She'd failed once more, only this time she'd failed her own best friend, and Grundy had seized the opportunity to get rid of Pearl. Jeanmarie pleaded, but Dr. Werner had silenced her. She was the one who should have been punished, not Pearl.

Dr. Werner had said, "temporarily," but Jeanmarie felt as if not weeks but months stretched before them. Nothing could be worse. There was no laughter that night, no shared jokes in the dormitory. Stunned disbelief at first had turned to anger and then to a heaviness that sat over all of them. Pearl said almost nothing.

In the dark Jeanmarie and Winnie had traded beds and pushed Pearl's close to Jeanmarie's. Jeanmarie didn't know how late it was, but across the room Winnie snored lightly, and the twins breathed evenly; only she and Pearl lay awake. "It won't be for long," Jeanmarie whispered. "It can't be. When Mrs. Ripple comes back she'll understand and help us." Under her breath she prayed, "Please, Lord, let her come soon and help us."

Mrs. Ripple hadn't come. Instead at noon a phone call from Dr. Werner came. He had found a place, a special school for the blind who would take Pearl for the time being. "Now that's as it should be," Miss Grundy pronounced. "He will be picking you up in the morning at 9:00 sharp. You'll need to pack your things and be ready. He's sending 'round a suitcase for you." Jeanmarie held Pearl's hand as if her heart would stop if she let go.

When the suitcase arrived late in the afternoon, Miss Grundy handed it to Jeanmarie. "Guess you might as well finish the job, Miss," she said. Jeanmarie took it without a word. She could not look at her.

The suitcase held most of Pearl's earthly goods—two changes of clothes, socks, a pair of slippers, a nightgown, shorts, a swimsuit, a few keepsakes, and a sweater. "If I need my winter clothes, I'll let you know," Pearl said.

"You won't need them; you won't," Jeanmarie protested. "I wish we'd kept walking yesterday and never come back," she said. It wasn't fair.

"How far would we have gotten?" Pearl said. She felt again for the stamped, addressed envelope Jeanmarie had given her to mail back as soon as she knew the address of the new place. Carefully she tucked it inside her suitcase under the sweater. Her pencil and pen she stuffed into the toe of a slipper. "That's it."

"One thing more," Jeanmarie said. She took the wooden cross from her neck, turned it over, and looked at the initials M. G. "I know she would have wanted you to have this; me too. *Vaya con Dios,*" she whispered. "Friends stick together, and we will. I'll write, so don't worry. If I don't hear from you, I'll find a way to get the address from Dr. Werner." She hugged Pearl hard. "It can't be for long; it won't be."

Pearl hugged her back, then slipped the cross over her head. "Thanks. It sort of feels right. I wonder if poor Nellie ever remembers?" Pearl felt for her towel and bar of soap. "I'll take my bath now. I know the way."

Jeanmarie watched her go, feeling from the bed to the closet, to the dresser, to the door, and out into the hall, turning left along the wall. Pearl *did* know the way. They'd practiced the bath routine, and she knew that as well. If only the pot holder hadn't caught fire none of this would be happening. If only Jeanmarie hadn't suggested walking on the tracks they'd never have needed to come back into the cottage. Impulsive, she'd done it again! Jeanmarie sat where she was on the edge of the iron cot. She felt heavy, like Pilgrim, whose picture in the book *Pilgrim's Progress* showed him bent under a heavy bundle strapped to his back.

"I don't understand, God; why must Pearl be blind?" She thought of the cross, of the young girl who had died, and then of Nellie. She wiped her face and felt wetness. "It isn't fair," she whispered. What good had the cross done them? Maria had died, Nellie was sick, Pearl was blind, and they'd all worn it. "I don't understand," she said.

In the bathroom, Pearl ran the water, felt it, and turned off the faucet. For a long time she sat on the floor, her forehead resting against the edge of the tub. "I don't understand, dear God, and I don't want to be blind. I want to stay here in the orphanage." She wept freely now. After a while she raised her head and wiped her face.

Trust and a thankful heart, the princess had said. Pearl wanted to trust and be thankful, but how could she? She fingered the cross on her neck. "I am thankful," she whispered. "I can think, and I can walk and talk, and some people don't have that much. And I'll try, God. I know that wherever I go, no one can keep you out or hide me from you; so I guess I really am going with you." She fingered the cross around her neck and whispered, *"Vaya con Dios."*

The bandages itched. It couldn't hurt to take them off. Anyway, she didn't want to get them wet, and she should wash her hair. She undid them layer after layer and let them drop. The light was so bright she covered her eyes. Bright? Slowly, she took away her fingers and looked at the bathtub, the sink, the walls. Trembling, she stood up and looked into the mirror above the sink. "It's true; I can see!" she screamed. "Thank you, God, thank you!" Still trembling she raced down the hall and into the dorm to an astonished Jeanmarie.

Almost a week had gone by. Finished early with her chores Jeanmarie slipped into the cellar and out the back door. In the small woods near the cottage she found a thick maple. Safely hidden from sight of anyone in Wheelock she sat with her back against its thick trunk. Morning sun had already dried the wet grass. Her cotton dress felt cool under the green branches that spread above her like a canopy. The sweet smell of wild phlox tickled her nose as she unfolded several sheets of notepaper and began writing. Two envelopes lay beside her. She had almost finished when footsteps came hurrying toward her. Pearl. She'd known where to find her.

Pearl's freckled face with its beaming smile told Jeanmarie the news was good. "I'm back," she said. "Passed every exam perfectly. The doctor says he doesn't understand it, but everything is just fine."

Jeanmarie smiled and held up her fingers in a V for victory sign. "That's great."

Hitching up the skirt of her white summer dress, Pearl plunked down beside her. "What are you writing?"

Jeanmarie looked up with another smile. "That one near the envelope is for Wilfred. I'm sure someone will read it to him since he can't with both arms in casts. This one is for Nellie." Her face grew serious. "All she wanted was a friend. And friends stick, don't they?" She looked at Pearl's glowing face. "Like us," she said.

Pearl leaned forward and slipped off the cross. "Here," she said. "Send it to her. Maybe it will help. It's what friends do."

Jeanmarie placed the cross in the envelope, signed her note to Nellie, "Jeanmarie, with love," folded it, and put it in with the cross. *"Vaya con Dios,"* she whispered.

More about This Book

During World War II the Ringling Brothers and Barnum and Bailey Greatest Show on Earth entertained audiences with grand patriotic displays. Sadly, only one month after the D-Day landings in Normandy and the start of the Allied invasion of Hitler's Europe, the great circus itself suffered the worst fire in circus history.

The Big Top, the world's largest tent, 600 feet long and 200 feet wide, held 12,000 people. Because of the war and the shortage of fireproof canvas, the almost new tent had been coated with a waterproof mixture of paraffin and benzene, which ignited quickly and burned rapidly. On the day of the fire a crowd of 6,789 people attended the show. Emmet Kelley, in his Weary Willie clown costume, and the Great Wallenda family high-wire performers were about to perform when the circus band began playing "Stars and Stripes Forever," the circus signal to clear the tent. The fire spread quickly, and in the panic many lives were taken and many people were injured. Several showed great courage in acts of heroism like the circus band members who played until the last tent pole fell crashing into their bandstand, forcing them to flee. Outside, the men continued to play, hoping to calm the dazed crowds.

In *Jeanmarie, with Love*, though the location is changed for the sake of the story, the circus fire is based on the actual one in 1944 in Hartford. As in the real event, hospitals and hundreds of volunteers responded to the needs of those caught in the fire. In Jeanmarie's story, Bellevue Hospital plays a major part in the rescue work.

Bellevue Hospital, a free hospital to those who could not pay, was the largest city hospital in the world. Buildings added to the original hospital were already old and outdated by the time of World War II. Student interns truly could lose their way in its endless corridors. The war brought hardships to the hospital too as Bellevue-trained nurses were considered the best, and many left to serve their country. The hospital was also famous for its advances in medicine, and in Jeanmarie's time some of the best medical care was at Bellevue. Frequently the circus put on a performance for the patients, and in return circus workers in need of a hospital found a warm reception at Bellevue. In *Jeanmarie, with Love,* I could think of no more exciting place for a young orphan girl to have her appendix removed. The adventure that followed seemed well suited to Bellevue, a hospital that still exists in New York City.

Lucille Travis, writer, speaker, and former English teacher, enjoys visiting historic sites and researching old documents. She is the author of several books for children and lives with her husband in St. Paul, Minnesota.

Also Available . . .

MYSTERIES
0-8010-4471-5
$5.99

In *Jeanmarie and the FBI*, the orphans' curiosity gets the best of them. Friendships grow as the orphans work together to uncover a World War II spy and find themselves kidnapped with little hope of escape. Jeanmarie and her friends discover that people aren't always who they seem to be—and that God is the only one who can protect them.

Also Available . . .

APPLE VALLEY MYSTERIES

0-8010-4470-7
$5.99

In *Jeanmarie and the Runaways,* the orphans learn a real-life social studies lesson. When Jeanmarie finds orphaned migrant kids Juan and Serena, she's determined to help them hide from the evil Don Carlos. But when her plan backfires, Jeanmarie's last hope is telling the truth. The orphans learn the hard way that honesty is *always* the best policy.